HIDDEN ASSETS

HIDDEN ASSETS

•

Barbara Meyers
and
Marlene Stringer

AVALON BOOKS
NEW YORK

Mey

PRINTED IN THE UNITED STATES OF AMERICA
ON ACID-FREE PAPER
BY HADDON CRAFTSMEN, BLOOMSBURG, PENNSYLVANIA

Barbara Meyers:

For my soul mates, Kevin and Cathy

Marlene Stringer:

For Neil, who believed, and with thanks to Harriet Shannon,
Roslyn Stringer and Janet Warhaftig

The authors especially thank
Marilyn Prather and Jasmine Cresswell

Chapter One

Liz savored each deep breath of the cool morning air during her two-mile jog. Soon enough she'd be behind her desk at the library, struggling with budget cuts and cost projections for the children's new reading program. She'd spearheaded this literacy campaign all year—she couldn't allow the bean counters to refuse funding for her pet project.

She paused to calculate her heart rate. With two fingers pressed to her throat she counted out ten seconds, then walked the rest of the way to cool down.

"Morning, Ms. Brady."

Finished with her count, she grinned as Jimmy Duffy pedaled toward her, his bicycle basket stuffed with newspapers.

She grinned. "Jimmy, my man. What's the play this morning?"

Jimmy coasted, checking over his shoulder for approaching cars. There were none. "Go long to a count of five, hang three steps left." He yanked a rolled newspaper out of the basket.

Liz took off, counted to five, turned, took the planned three steps. The newspaper sailed into her hands. She tucked it under one arm and ran, dodging an overturned tricycle in one yard and a birdbath in the next, and hurdled the hedge onto her own lawn.

She did a victory dance as Jimmy followed on his bike, tossing newspapers right and left onto driveways.

"We're three for three this week," she reminded him as he glided past.

He gave her another grin. "We'll make the playoffs this season for sure."

Liz laughed. "See you tomorrow, Jimmy."

"See you tomorrow."

Flushed from her run, a smile on her face, Liz unlocked the front door and stepped inside. She rifled through the paper quickly, scanning the headlines before she showered. A picture in the society section caught her attention, and her smile died.

But Randy Hollander continued to smile at her—as did the woman next to him. His fiancée. Liz's good mood evaporated as she stared at the frozen image of her two-timing ex-boyfriend. Randy had been the last in a long line of good-looking, good-for-nothing-else men she'd dated.

After Randy, Liz quit playing by the old rules. She stopped emphasizing her looks to attract men. In fact, she made every effort to downplay each physical attribute. Her plan to find a man attracted to her mind instead of her body worked well. Too well. She hadn't had a real date in at least six months.

She groaned as she picked up a pen and set to work on Randy's picture, drawing in horns and blackening out teeth with a vengeance.

Just wait until her mother saw the newspaper. Vivian Brady would have several choice comments.

Liz let herself in the back door of the neat brick house and sniffed. She unwound the amber scarf from her neck, and pulled off her oversized gray sweater. Still Vivian didn't greet her.

Two slices of blackened bread popped abruptly from the toaster.

"Mom?"

"Hmmm?"

"Are you having your toast well-done this morning?"

Vivian Brady turned a page of the *Daily Eagle.* She carefully folded the newspaper along the columnar line and moved a ruler down a line of print without looking up at her daughter.

"Toast? Oh, it's the darkness control again." She frowned vaguely at the contrary appliance.

Pushing her horn-rimmed glasses farther up her nose, Liz glanced over Vivian's shoulder and sighed with relief. Her mother was scanning the classifieds—not the society section.

"Mom?"

"Hmmm?"

"You haven't even looked at me since I walked through the door. How about some coffee?"

"Oh, I'm sorry, Liz," Vivian smiled charmingly at her daughter. "Of course I'll sit with you. It's taken longer than I thought to get through all of these.

"It's been a while since I've searched through the classifieds," she confided. "Kind of lost my touch, if you know what I mean," she tore open a packet of sweetener, "and I'm not too familiar with these personal ads."

How, Liz wondered, *could I sneak out of here with the society section of my mother's newspaper without her even noticing?*

"By the way, I noticed Randy Hollander's engaged," Vivian said. She patted her well-coiffed ash blond hair and fixed Liz with a look.

Too late, Liz thought, trapped by her mother's steady gaze like a butterfly in a net.

"You should move on with your life as well, dear. Find someone new. Randy obviously did."

She stirred her coffee with a graceful flick of the wrist. Vivian took a tiny sip of her coffee. "I'll find someone for you," she vowed.

"Please don't concern yourself with the state of my social life," Liz warned in a gentle tone.

"Your social life is virtually non-existent. I'm your mother—of course I'm concerned," she told her daughter. "I want you to be happy."

"I am happy, Mother," insisted Liz between clenched teeth. "Being happy doesn't mean I have to be married. I don't have to date."

"Pooh," said Vivian, as if Liz's objection was nothing more than an annoying mosquito buzzing nearby. "How do you expect to meet a suitable man if you don't date?"

"Could we please not have this conversation?" Liz tried.

"Of course, dear." Vivian reached across and patted Liz's hand. "Now, then." She set her reading glasses on her nose and studied the classified section she'd brought to the table with her.

"I've been going through these personal ads—"

"Personal ads! You've got to be kidding." Liz stared at her mother.

"Just listen to this one, Liz," Vivian insisted. "He sounds perfect for you. SW/CM. Do you know what those letters stand for, dear?" Vivian looked over the paper at Liz.

Single Woman/Crazy Mother, Liz thought. She'd need to fortify herself with more than coffee this morning. "It stands for single, white, Christian male."

"Oh." Vivian took a split second to absorb this information before she continued to read. "Thirty-eight, never married . . ."

"There's a red flag for you," mumbled Liz, as she dabbed her chin with a starched napkin. Vivian did not believe in paper napkins.

Over the top of the newspaper her mother frowned at the interruption. "Spontaneous," she continued.

"That means unreliable," countered Liz.

"Seeking to explore inner self with the right woman."

"He's selfish and needs a surrogate mother."

"Under 35," Vivian emphasized in response.

Liz snorted. "He doesn't want a woman with too much mileage."

"Enjoys success . . ."

"Whose? He probably wants her to pay his way," Liz declared.

". . . dining out."

"Likes to eat. I'll bet he's . . . portly."

"Walks in the moonlight, quiet talks."

"Euphemisms for cheap dates. No, Mom. No way." She eyed her mother suspiciously. "What makes you think this guy is my dream date?"

Vivian shook her head in exasperation. "I like the tone of the ad." Vivian looked only slightly abashed. "He must be romantic, mentioning moonlight and quiet talks. Besides," she reminded Liz with a shake of her finger and a ring of determination in her voice, "it's only three weeks until the awards banquet. Finally my daughter will get some recognition. After all your hard work for the literacy campaign, you deserve it. But I still haven't heard who you're going with. I thought perhaps . . ."

Liz held up her hand. "No. I'd rather go alone than with an escort you set me up with. And I'm certainly not going out with someone from the personal ads. You're wasting your time, Mom."

"Listen to your mother, Liz. Big moments in life are much better shared with someone. You can't go alone."

"Forget it, Mother." Perhaps for Christmas she'd

give her mother a new dictionary. Though as far as Liz knew, the meaning of the word "no" hadn't changed in the past thousand years or so.

"Well, if you didn't care for that one, how about this . . . 'Tall, dark and handsome, DWM with BMW.' " Vivian paused. "He's a professional, Liz. You know you've always loved animals. He even has an advanced degree."

"A what?"

"He's a DWM. A veterinarian. With a BMW. Some extra training, I'm sure. Maybe he's a specialist."

A specialist my eye, Liz thought. *Not unless he specializes in women foolish and shallow enough to answer his ad.* She absolutely refused to encourage her mother. Vivian was already in over her head. "It's a car, Mother, not a degree."

"You mean he's a mechanic, not a veterinarian?"

Liz raised her eyes heavenward and silently prayed for patience. "Mom, first of all, when you see 'DWM' in the personals it means divorced, white male."

"Oh." That caught Vivian off-guard, but in seconds she regrouped. "But BMW—that's something good, right?"

"It's a car, Mother. Made in Germany. He drives a foreign import. Probably to impress women, or to compensate for some . . . shortfall." The lost expression on Vivian's face indicated that further explanation would be wasted. Liz sighed in resignation. "Never mind, Mom."

Liz knew her mother wouldn't give up easily, but she grew encouraged when Vivian tossed the newspaper aside and stood to refill their coffee cups. "Well, you know Liz, I'd be happy to screen appropriate candidates for you. It's your own fault you don't have a date for the banquet." Vivian indicated Liz's outfit with a frown and a thrust of her delicate chin. "Darling, you have a closet full of beautiful clothes, yet you wear such dowdy outfits! It's so unflattering. If you're going to wear that style, at least buy something that fits. This corduroy thing is at least two sizes too big for you."

"Don't you get it, Mom? I've changed the rules. My last boyfriend traded me in for a newer, younger model. I no longer dress to attract men. I have to go," she added, as she glanced at the clock.

She placed her dishes in the sink and looked over at her mother. Liz knew she hadn't inflicted any serious damage to her mother's feelings, nor to whatever alternate plan she was hatching in that lovely but devious head of hers.

"Are you going out today? Do you want to meet me for lunch?" asked Liz.

"Absolutely, darling. See you at one," Vivian replied, composed as always in her pale mint cashmere twinset and pearls.

Just a few blocks from her mother's house, the public library stood on a pretty, tree-lined street, located near the downtown shops and restaurants. Next door, the local YMCA provided a non-stop stream of traffic, and made the library a popular destination for all ages. It was in the heart of the town's recreational area.

Liz usually walked the few blocks from her house to the library, both for the exercise and the view. Occasionally she stopped by her mother's house on the way. Lately, though, each visit to Vivian's left her feeling like a twelve-year-old instead of a competent, independent adult. Her mother humored her, as she had during Liz's childhood. Liz could protest as loudly and as often as she wanted, but to no avail. Vivian knew what was best for Liz, whether Liz agreed or not.

This morning proved no different. She mentally reviewed all Vivian's past attempts to "fix her up." She shuddered at the memories. Vivian always produced an escort whenever one was needed rather than leave Liz to her own devices. From the teen canteen in junior high to her cousin's wedding two years ago, very little had changed. Her mother simply became more creative as Liz got older.

Liz didn't need her mother's help. Why couldn't her mother understand?

As she walked up the stone steps to the library, maple leaves crunched beneath her feet. She inhaled the crisp autumn air. Her mother was right about one thing—the gala dinner, her big night, was just around the corner.

"Good morning!" Cindy's enthusiastic greeting interrupted Liz's thoughts. Cindy Lewis was a longtime friend and fellow librarian. Tall and blond, she dressed impeccably and was lovely to behold.

"You look a bit frazzled this morning." Cindy eyed the bulge of printouts in Liz's overstuffed leather satchel. Liz plopped the bag onto the counter with a thud and rubbed her shoulder.

"Not letting the bureaucrats get to you, are you?"

"Not exactly," sighed Liz. "I'm sure I can find the additional funding for the children's literacy project. Wouldn't it be ironic if the program they give me an award for this year gets cut from next year's budget?"

"I know you won't let that happen," Cindy replied with confidence. "Everything else okay?"

"It's my mother. She's out hunting big game again."

"Oh, no," said Cindy, covering her mouth in mock horror. Her voice dropped to a stage whisper as she covered her cheeks with her hands. "Not," she gasped, "stalking the elusive Great American Blind Date?"

Liz nodded miserably. "This morning she reviewed the personal ads for me. You'd think she'd keep her mission a secret, but she doesn't even bother to destroy incriminating evidence! She even offered to screen a selection of appropriate possibilities. The *personals,* Cindy! My own mother is convinced that my salvation lies in dating complete strangers!"

"She wants you to be happy," Cindy assured Liz. "It goes with the job description of 'mother'. And she might have a point, you know. Your new look isn't exactly flattering." Cindy eyed the loose-fitting, over-sized jumper which fell well past Liz's calves. "It leaves *everything* to the imagination. And that awful sweater really has to go."

Liz looked down at her sweater. Even she had to admit it was much too large, but it was like an old friend, comforting and always there when she needed it.

"Your hair is beautiful, but you always wear it up. I would kill for a natural wave like you have. Why don't you do something besides pile it up on top of your head? You're certainly giving Sally a run for her money." Liz didn't care for the uncomplimentary comparison to their sixty-ish colleague, Sally Henson, who gave new meaning to the term frumpy.

"I no longer buy into the whole vanity thing." Liz turned and tried to make out her reflection in the glass enclosure that held the official notices inside. "I don't think I look that bad, do I?" She turned back to Cindy.

"Even nuns retired their habits twenty years ago, Liz. You used to turn every male head in sight. Now you look like a disastrous 'before' image in a fashion magazine. Sometimes even I'm hard-pressed to recognize you as the friend I knew six months ago. Tell you what, Halloween is in a couple of weeks. Wear some of your old clothes. You know—ones that fit. Like the black designer suit. It will be the perfect disguise."

"Have you been talking to my mother? Her focus went right from my outfit to the awards dinner. She insists I can't attend alone."

"I wish I knew someone suitable," Cindy said sympathetically, "but everyone in my circle is already attached."

"This feels like my high school prom all over again,

you know? I *have* to go, and if I don't have a date, my life will be over. Period. Fifteen years later and I'm supposed to panic just like in high school. No date for the big dance. It sure doesn't feel like progress."

Chapter Two

Evan Delaford pushed away his soup bowl as a young blond waitress appeared. "May I take that, sir?" She refilled his coffee cup and cleared the lunch dishes.

The restaurant waitstaff hustled between packed tables while impatient customers vied for the next available seats. Even the hostess pitched in and bussed an empty table.

Evan made a few notes about the restaurant operation on a yellow legal pad.

He took a sip of coffee and removed *The New York Times Book Review* from his briefcase.

Just as he finished the review of John Grisham's latest, a woman slid into the seat across from him.

"Okay, we don't have much time." She glanced furtively around. "My daughter thinks I'm in the restroom. Like I told you on the phone, if she thinks I have anything to do with setting her up, she won't give you the time of day, so whatever you do, don't let on I answered your ad."

"Excuse me—" Evan tried to interrupt.

"She's over there, the second table from the window. See her?"

He turned his head slightly to get a better view. "Don't look! Don't look!" the woman hissed.

His attention snapped back to her and he started to grin. "Sorry."

Without turning his head, Evan chanced a quick glance in the daughter's direction. From this angle all he could see was a partial profile, but something about the tendrils of dark hair escaping from a tightly wound bun, and the curve of her jaw intrigued him.

"I'm sorry, Mrs . . . ?"

"Brady, of course. Vivian Brady." Her lips tightened. "You must have had quite a response to your ad, then. Just exactly how many meetings do you have set up for today?"

"Excuse me?"

"You told me you'd never done this before," Vivian Brady pointed out.

"I haven't," Evan insisted. "I didn't."

"We just spoke yesterday, but you don't remember my name." She nodded at the legal pad near his elbow. "Perhaps you should write things down. I find it helps."

"Look, Mrs. Brady, there's been a mistake. I'm not the man you think I am."

"Oh, yes you are. Do you have any idea what it took for me to set this up? You haven't even met her." The woman appeared positively desperate, so Evan softened his approach.

"I'm not here because of the personal ads," he told her gently.

"Of course you are. You're in the right restaurant at the right time. You told me you'd have *The New York Times Book Review* on the table. You can't back out on me now."

"I wasn't going to back out," Evan began, not quite sure how he'd even gotten in.

Vivian Brady reached across the table and patted his hand. "I know this is awkward. But I'm sure you'll like Liz once you get to know her."

Evan darted another glance in Liz's direction. As Evan watched, she picked up her nearly empty water glass. The ice in the bottom of the glass plummeted toward her mouth. Several cubes popped out into her lap; one escaped over her shoulder. She set the glass down and calmly dabbed at the dribble of water on her chin. Deftly she scooped up the wayward cubes within her reach and returned her attention to her reading material. From this distance it almost looked like *The New York Times Book Review. Hmmm. . . . why not?*

He'd be in southern Illinois checking out restaurant chains for his investors, anyway. There were times, especially in the evenings, when he welcomed a diversion. Sharing a meal with a small-town frump would be preferable to dining alone. But first he needed to clear up this misunderstanding. Slowly he turned his attention back to the woman's mother.

"It's not that, Mrs. Brady, it's—"

"Now don't mind the way Liz is dressed. I've told her those clothes don't flatter her. And that sweater!" Vivian Brady sighed. "She's never without it. It's a phase she's going through, something about finding a man who's interested in her mind."

"Mrs. Brady—"

She raced on. "You obviously read, so you should know better than to judge a book by its cover."

"I wasn't judging her," Evan defended himself. "What I'm trying to tell you is—"

"Could you turn your head?" Vivian interrupted.

Obligingly, Evan turned his head to the right.

"Hmmm." Vivian Brady leaned forward, grasped his chin in her hand and gently turned his head in the other direction.

What's next? Evan wondered.

"You need a haircut."

"I probably do," he agreed.

"I just remembered one of Liz's rules," she told him, still studying him. "Let's forget it," Vivian blurted.

"Excuse me?" She had mistakenly handed him the opportunity to meet the mysterious Liz, and now abruptly snatched it away?

"It won't work. You're too good-looking. Why didn't you mention that on the phone?"

"I—I—" Had he just been flattered, or insulted?

"Another one of Liz's rules," Vivian said. "She

doesn't date good-looking men. Won't give them the time of day. Not after the fiasco with Randy." She sighed. "It's too bad, really, because otherwise you sounded perfect for her." She looked once again at the *Book Review*. "I'll pay for your lunch," she told him, reaching into her purse. "I'm sorry this was such a waste of time for both of us."

"Wait!" Evan nearly shouted. He hadn't even met this Liz person, but for some reason he now wanted to. "Let me just introduce myself to her, okay?"

Liz's mother studied him a moment longer before she shrugged and picked up the check. She slid gracefully out of the booth and nodded in her daughter's direction. "You're on your own. I'll give you five minutes."

Frank McCourt's new book was a must-read, Liz Brady decided as she perused the best-sellers. She looked at the fiction list once again, noticing the new books by a couple of her favorite authors. Which to purchase out of her carefully hoarded monthly book-buying budget? Unable to decide, she turned back to the previous page.

"Excuse me."

Liz's gaze traveled up, up, up, from a pair of well-manicured masculine hands wrapped around the handle of a glossy black leather briefcase, to a set of twinkling blue eyes. Somehow she managed to take in everything in-between: the expensive pinstriped gray suit, the neatly knotted silk tie beneath the starched white collar. A cleanly shaven square jaw, sensual lips, dark brown hair (just a shade too long), brushed back and curling slightly over his collar.

"Are you finished with your salad?"

The salad bowl in front of her was nearly empty. She adjusted her glasses and took a good look at him. He was much too well dressed to be a busboy. Still, he seemed interested in her leftovers. "The crouton and that one wilted lettuce leaf are yours, if that's what you're after."

His quick easy smile, revealing a flash of even white teeth, had the effect of a starburst on Liz. She felt compelled to watch for another one.

"Actually, as appealing as that is, I'd like to ask you a few questions."

"Am I under arrest?" Liz raised an eyebrow.

He rewarded her with another quick smile. "No, no, it's about the salad."

Her eyes flickered over the bowl. "*It's* under arrest?"

This time he chuckled, picked up the conversational ball she tossed him and bantered. "No, but it is part of an ongoing investigation." He indicated the empty chair across from her. "May I?"

Liz glanced around. *Where* had her mother disappeared to? "Just for a minute."

"Now then, about the salad," he began.

She held up a hand. "Really, Officer, I've never seen this salad before today."

"Uh-huh." He withdrew a yellow legal pad from the briefcase and a gold pen from his breast pocket.

"And how would you say the salad presented it-self?"

"Just as an ordinary chef's salad. There was really nothing in it to arouse suspicion."

"Nothing special about it?"

"Well, you know, lots of lettuce, hard-boiled egg slices, shredded ham and turkey, cheese, tomato—"

"What about the dressing?"

"Ah, the dressing. The creamy Parmesan. It was imitation Parmesan, right? I knew it!" She snapped her fingers as if she had just solved the crime of the century.

Liz smiled. She was enjoying this.

He slid a business card across the table to her. *Evan Delaford*, it read. *Investments, Business Consultant, Venture Capitalist.* A Chicago address.

"Oh," she whispered, looking up from the card. "So you're working undercover?"

"Yes." He leaned across the table. "A possibility of restaurant franchising, you know. Very hush-hush."

Liz nodded. This had to be the most original pick-up routine ever.

"We're currently recruiting civilians to assist with our investigation. I could use your help," he went on in the same hushed tone of voice. "You do eat on a regular basis, don't you?"

She nodded, trying hard not to giggle.

"Anything besides salad?"

"If it will help the cause," she assured him.

"You understand, this is strictly for research purposes. I'll have to interrogate you after each course."

She raised her right hand. "I understand completely."

"Shall we rendezvous here tomorrow night, say at around nineteen-hundred hours?"

Liz hesitated. She gave him the quick once-over, which she'd perfected over the years. No sign of a wedding band and no obvious indication that one had recently encircled his ring finger. The only hint of jewelry was a sleek gold watch discreetly hidden beneath a starched white cuff.

She hadn't been out to dinner in ages, but the restaurant was familiar territory. Her mother would be ecstatic. "I'll be here," Liz agreed, still amused. He stood. "Should I wear a disguise?" she inquired.

He took in the baggy sweater and the oversized glasses. "I think the one you have on will do."

Chapter Three

"Okay, okay, so it's not a date. What are you wearing?"

Liz gazed at herself critically in the full-length mirror. "My red dress," she mumbled.

She didn't miss Kate's sigh. Conversations with her younger sister could, at times, be even worse than those with her mother. "Which red one? The awful burgundy that hangs on you?"

Liz smiled. "Of course not. This is the red crepe, the one with the little white flowers on it. It even has a belt."

"Oh, great! I thought I told you Nana has the same dress in blue. I don't know what your problem is— you used to have the greatest wardrobe."

I still do, Liz thought, glancing toward her packed closet. "Look, Kate, I spent my twenties dressing to

21

attract men, and it worked. Problem was, all they wanted was my body. I plan to spend my thirties finding someone who values me for my brain. I don't expect you to understand, little sis." *How could she?* Liz wondered. *Kate was only twenty-six. She had lots of time before Vivian took charge of her social life.*

"And what if your plan doesn't work, Pooker?" she asked, resorting to her childhood nickname for her older sister. "What's the strategy for your forties?"

Liz laughed with a nonchalance she didn't feel. "By then my biological alarm clock will have been beaten into submission, I'll be hauling all the important parts of my body behind me, and I'll be brain-dead from Mom's nagging. Are you happy now?"

"You're not wearing that gray sweater, are you?" Kate asked.

Liz considered shrugging out of the offending article quickly so she could truthfully answer no, but Kate beat her to the punch.

"You can't wear that old rag, Liz! Not on a date."

In truth, in the past half-year or so, Liz had grown attached to her security blanket. It concealed, she believed, some of her more attractive physical attributes. "It's not a date, Kate, I told you. This evening is more like a—a business meeting."

"But you're going to dinner."

"Yes, but I'm meeting him there. He's not picking me up."

"It's still dinner out. With a man." Kate enjoyed stating the obvious.

A very good-looking man, Liz thought. She hated

the part of herself which tempted her to change into something a bit more date-like. The comfortable print dress was long and loose. Her well-worn flats were her favorite pair of shoes. Maybe some lip gloss . . .

"What about make-up?" Kate wanted to know.

Liz snapped to attention as Kate unwittingly followed her train of thought long distance.

"Is Mom at your house?" she asked.

"Of course not, silly," Kate giggled. "What do you think, she sprouted wings and flew to Springfield this morning?"

Sprouted horns was more like it, like a stubborn ram bent on getting its way, Liz thought. She glanced away from the mirror to check her watch. "Nineteen hundred hours. That's seven o'clock, right? Military time?"

"Yes," Kate agreed. "And it's after six now. Liz, would you think about changing clothes? You *can* be attractive without flaunting yourself, you know."

"I suppose," Liz said, not entirely convinced.

"At least lose the sweater," Kate insisted.

"Okay." Liz opened her closet door. "I have to go."

Seated at the end of the bar, Evan Delaford noticed Liz before she saw him, and he was glad. He had time to study her before they were face to face. But what was she wearing? This get-up was even worse than the floppy dress and too-big sweater she'd worn yesterday. *Why did this woman insist on wearing clothes that didn't fit?* Evan wondered.

The matronly, high collared dress covered her from

neck to mid-calf in a flowing fabric. A long-sleeved navy jacket added to the camouflage, making him wonder once again what was hidden underneath. The outfit was all wrong, but the ugly clothes could not detract from her beauty. She had the creamy complexion models hunger for, and oversized glasses could not conceal her lively green eyes.

Evan suspected her hair was thick and wavy and probably fell past her shoulders, if it ever escaped the bun she seemed so fond of wearing. What was she hiding from? A man would have to be blind not to notice her figure—a tiny waist and generous curves in all the right places. *Disguise indeed,* Evan thought as he made his way toward her. *They would see who was fooling whom.*

I'm having a good time, Liz thought halfway through the meal. *How can this be?*

True, as Evan Delaford had warned, he quizzed her about every morsel of food and cross-examined her about the drink. Did the ice tea have too much sugar? Was the lemon rind twisted to her satisfaction?

From there they proceeded to an onion appetizer, deep fried in spicy batter, served with a horseradish sauce. The questions never ended. Was it excessively greasy? The batter too heavy? Too highly seasoned?

The salad was literally picked apart by Evan as he asked questions and made notes. Liz sat back and smiled.

"What?" He asked, giving her a suspicious glance.

"You take your work very seriously, don't you?"

He shrugged, toying with a bite of his own salad. "Making recommendations on what other people do with their money is not something I take lightly, if that's what you're asking." He glanced around the crowded restaurant, which was now intimately dimmed. "Do you think a place like this would succeed in an average American city?"

"I don't know why not," Liz returned. "I'm enjoying myself." Liz had a clear impression that there was a computer-like brain behind those to-die-for blue eyes and chiseled cheekbones.

There must be something wrong with him. If she guessed right, he was in his early thirties and still unattached. How many red flags lurked behind his nearly perfect exterior?

"Hi, Liz. Fancy meeting you here!"

Both Liz and Evan looked up as a pretty blond bumped against their table. Liz forced a smile. "Hi, Cindy." She glanced at Evan. "Cindy Lewis, Evan Delaford. Cindy works with me at the library," she informed Evan.

Evan stood and shook hands with Cindy. Liz hated the instant flash of irritation she felt when he turned his charming smile on the other woman. *Knock it off,* she warned her subconscious. *This is a business meeting, not a date.*

What Liz liked about Cindy was that she took her stunning looks for granted, chalking them up to genetics, nothing more. Besides, Cindy was lucky enough to find a man who valued her brain *and* her beauty, and was very happily married.

"You look familiar," Cindy mused as she tapped one perfectly manicured nail against her chin and studied Evan.

"Really?" Evan shot a glance Liz's way. "I can't imagine why."

"Hmmm. Me neither," Cindy agreed. "But I know I've seen you somewhere."

When neither Liz nor Evan commented, Cindy took the hint. "I see Nick giving me the evil eye." Cindy waved to her husband. "See you tomorrow, Liz." She gave Evan another once-over. "Nice meeting you, Evan."

"I thought you'd never been to Rockleigh," Liz remarked as Cindy disappeared into the crowd near the bar.

"I haven't," Evan agreed.

"Then why is she so sure she's seen you before?" Liz asked. The city of Rockleigh stood just across the Mississippi River from Missouri in southern Illinois. It wasn't so small a place that everyone knew everyone else, but it wasn't so big that a visit from anyone as sophisticated as Evan Delaford would go completely unnoticed.

"Perhaps she's mistaken. Ah, here's our dinner." Seemingly impervious to the perky waitress, he smoothly changed the subject, but he didn't fool Liz for a minute. Cindy had a near photographic memory when it came to faces. If she said she'd seen Evan Delaford before tonight, she probably had. Evan hadn't denied the possibility, either—he merely deflected the inquiry.

As the evening drew to a close, Liz was having trouble determining whether this was a social or a business encounter. Although Evan was certainly attentive to his research, he also paid attention to her. Unmistakable masculine attention, and it unnerved her. He listened closely and chuckled at her jokes.

"Well, that was fun," Evan said as they reached Liz's car.

"For a business meeting, yes it was," Liz agreed. "I hope it was helpful."

"Oh, it was more than helpful."

"Well, good. Glad I could be of service." *Be of service? Liz groaned. What am I, a clerk at Buy-and-Save? Thank you for shopping with us. Come back soon now, you hear?*

"Would you be willing to do this again?"

"Do what?" Liz asked. They hadn't *done* anything.

"Have dinner with me. I've got three more restaurants to check out."

"Oh," Liz said. At least she now had their relationship defined—it was strictly business. Just the way she wanted it. Why then was she so disappointed?

"Sure," she responded. "Why not?"

"I'll call you then?" Evan sounded uncertain, as though he couldn't quite believe she agreed to have dinner with him again.

"Fine." He had no ulterior motive. Evan needed an assistant, a dinner companion to help him with his research. Afterwards, he would head back to Chicago, prepared to make a recommendation to his investors on whether or not to back the operation.

Then why did her heart flutter as he stepped closer? Was he going to kiss her? Did she want him to? Yes. No. Yes. This was supposed to be strictly business. Still, the evening had had a lingering undertone which smacked of a "date." Evan leaned forward. He *was* going to kiss her. Or try to. His fingers brushed hers. Her car keys slipped from her grasp, landing with a jarring crash on the pavement.

Her car keys! In an unexpectedly chivalrous move, Evan had attempted to take them to unlock her car door. *Stupid,* she told herself, flustered for thinking he was going to kiss her. Were her thoughts obvious to him? She quickly bent down to retrieve her keys, trying to escape with some shred of dignity intact.

Thwack! Liz momentarily saw stars as her head collided with Evan's. She lost her balance before Evan could catch her, and landed with a plop in the only puddle in the entire parking lot. Her purse fell with a splash next to her, shooting a spray of dirty water into her face.

She sat there stunned, knees splayed, as Evan steadied himself against her car.

"Oh, Liz, I'm so sorry." He pressed one hand to his head and extended the other one out to her. She stood up, then bent to retrieve her purse, just as Evan did the same.

"Ouch!"

"Oof!" They cracked their already tender heads together in the same places and went down in a heap on wet asphalt. Oblivious to the stinging sensation in her elbow, Liz was conscious of only one thing: the heat of Evan's body on top of her, his heart beating next to hers.

"You're such a gentleman." She couldn't help smiling.

He lowered his head toward hers. He was going to kiss her! No, he wasn't. Yes, he was! Mirroring her confusion, Evan hesitated. The moment was gone. "Yeah," he agreed. "My good manners are deadly."

"Okay, wait a minute." He hauled himself to his feet. His pants were ripped and his knee was bleeding. "Nice and easy now," he instructed. Liz put her hands in his and got to her feet. Her elbow throbbed and she was unaccountably light-headed. Perhaps she was falling in love. Perhaps she had a concussion.

"I have a plan. You get the keys. I'll get your purse. Deal?"

Liz nodded and turned, spotting her keys nearby. She bent to retrieve them and felt her bottom connect with something reasonably hard, but definitely not a part of her car. It was Evan's rear. Liz stumbled and managed to right herself, but the unexpected impact threw Evan off balance. Again the rending sound of material as Evan landed on his uninjured knee, and the contents of Liz's purse went flying.

"Oh, no. Oh, Evan, I'm so sorry!" Liz stepped forward to help him, but Evan ducked his head and held up an arm to ward her off.

"No—don't—just stay where you are. I'll get this."

Liz watched helplessly as Evan gathered up her comb, loose change, breath mints and the rest, and dropped them back into her bag before rising to his feet. His pants legs were both ripped, the skin of his knees scraped raw from the rough pavement. The rest of him was slightly mud-spattered, his tie askew, hair disheveled. He looked like he'd crawled up a mountain without protective gear.

"Give me your keys." Keeping his distance, he held out his hand. Liz passed them over. Evan unlocked her car, opened the door and tossed her purse onto the passenger seat. He waited until she was safely behind the wheel before giving her the keys. "I'll call you."

"Okay, so who's this Evan Delaford character?" Cindy wanted to know the following morning. "And I thought you were off good-looking men after the fiasco with Randy Hollander. What's the deal?"

Cindy didn't miss a beat as she checked in books from the overnight drop. Liz winced at the mention of gorgeous Randy Hollander. She had almost convinced herself that Randy was in love with her before she realized that Randy was too in love with himself to care about anyone else.

On the surface, the man appeared to have it all. Looks, money, flashy car, rising career. Initially, Liz was willing to overlook Randy's short attention span and vacuous comments. It took her almost a year to realize there was very little substance between his well-shaped ears. So little, in fact, that he thought nothing of pursuing the cute redhead across the hall.

Liz decided she needed a man with a brain. A man with a heart. Maybe she could even find one with a little bit of courage. She wouldn't settle for less. The man of her dreams would be one who thought the way she did. If a man wanted her as window-dressing he was crossed off as a candidate. Contrary to her mother's opinion, Liz was sure she did not need make-up and fashionable clothes to make herself attractive. Even if her nails weren't polished, if she didn't fuss with her hair or wear contacts, Liz was positive there was a man out there somewhere who found her appealing anyway.

"Liz?" Cindy stopped checking in books and gave her a friendly nudge, jostling her out of her reverie. "What's the deal with Evan Delaford?" she asked again.

Liz shrugged and began stacking books onto a cart. How much could she reasonably tell Cindy without giving away Evan's business? "He's in town to check out some restaurants," she answered truthfully. "I met him in Goodtimes the other day, and he asked me to join him for dinner."

"What does he do exactly?"

She saw Cindy trying to piece together whatever Liz wasn't telling her. The icepack Liz administered her swollen scalp last night didn't really help—she had a bump the size of a small egg on top of her head, and her throbbing headache was immune to pain relievers. Liz wasn't up to answering any more questions about Evan Delaford.

"I'm really not sure. Investments or something, I think. Oh, my, look at the time. Better unlock the doors!" She grabbed her keys and breathed a sigh of relief. The less Cindy knew about her relationship with

Evan Delaford the better. Liz didn't need any reminders of her vow to stay away from men like him. Besides, after the way poor Evan limped away last night, she doubted he'd ask for her help again.

Chapter Four

"Yes?" Evan mumbled into the phone.

"Good morning, Mr. Delaford. It's seven o'clock. Have a nice day," replied the hotel operator.

"Thanks," he said, and turned over onto his back, enjoying the luxury of total silence.

In the few moments before full consciousness, Evan stretched out in the familiar unfamiliarity of his hotel bed. The question of which hotel in which city was irrelevant; they were all the same. He enjoyed good hotels; they played a huge role in his life and business. When all was said and done, he'd spent more time on the road in the past couple of years than at his magnificent apartment on Lakeshore Drive.

He often questioned how much he enjoyed spending time there alone, and the answer was always *not very.* The address was impeccable, the view terrific. At this

33

point he owned few furnishings, which didn't bother him, since the apartment didn't feel like home. Evan remembered the profile that appeared several months ago in a national magazine: "He lives a monastic lifestyle, despite his level of success. He's on the verge of becoming engaged to a great beauty, the former Miss Illinois, who's now queen of the Chicago morning news scene, Aileen Summers."

Well, he thought, *that relationship bit the dust.* So did all the others in the long line of Mrs. Delaford-wannabes, ever since he turned up on everyone's "A" list. *Money certainly added to one's assets,* he thought, *in more ways than one!*

He stretched. "Ow!" he moaned as he banged his head against the headboard. He tentatively explored the tender lump on his head. He turned over and groaned as his sore knees protested movement. Not since playing college rugby had he experienced a morning like this. He wondered whether Liz's head carried the same souvenir as his own, after their Keystone Cops routine of the previous evening.

Despite his pain, Evan found himself smiling as he stepped into the shower. He inhaled the steam and considered how often during the past couple of days he had thought about Liz Brady. *She would have added color and human interest to that profile piece,* he thought. He replaced the mental picture of him and Aileen with one of him and the small-town librarian with atrocious taste in clothes.

Whatever drove her to disguise her natural assets piqued his curiosity and added to the attraction. This was an unusual situation for him. Every other woman who came into contact with Evan Delaford over the last few years went out of her way to be as attractive and alluring as possible. He had heard tales of women resorting to plastic surgery to make themselves more appealing to him. They would stoop to the most outrageous ploys to meet him. He was one of the top ten bachelors on any list one cared to name—except Liz Brady's list. According to her mother, he wouldn't make her cut.

She was, quite simply, one of the most rational females he'd ever met, completely unfazed by his appearance and success. Unlike other women, a man's money and power seemed to leave her unimpressed.

Once or twice during dinner last night he caught a glimpse of the bright, beautiful woman hiding inside the awful clothes. Her wonderful thick chignon of almost-black hair beckoned him. He wanted to free it, feel it run through his fingers, while he held her tightly.

Like any other project that caught his attention, he would actively pursue further study. *If* Liz would let him. Her plain-Jane disguise must have something to do with some man, Evan mused.

He reached for his after-shave and almost applied a cologne given to him by Aileen, his ex-girlfriend. He recapped the bottle and tossed it in the trash—the fragrance was too floral and never appealed to him anyway.

Aileen had tried her best to change him, he admitted, thinking back over their months together. He was more of a workaholic robot than a human being, according to her. Still, Aileen could be fun at times, and he went along with her decisions on where they dined and with whom they socialized. He couldn't recall so many social invitations disguised as charity parties as he had in the six months they were a couple.

Aileen thrived in the spotlight. Her stint as Miss Illinois served her well, as did her television training. She chit-chatted and mingled with the best of them, while making certain her name was intimately linked with Evan's. She didn't mind keeping the competition at bay.

Evan quickly tired of the social lifestyle Aileen adored. It took time away from his investment research and from his clients.

So he purposely increased his business travel, and became discreetly unavailable to escort Aileen around town. After a while, items hinting at a break-up appeared in the local gossip columns, and Aileen reluctantly accepted the obvious. She was fairly gracious about their split in public. *Who wouldn't be,* he wondered, *with a parting gift of a diamond bracelet?* Yet he knew she hadn't accepted his decision as final.

The ringing of the phone interrupted his unpleasant train of thought.

"Yes?"

"Evan? Is that you?"

"Yes, Paul, it's me. What's wrong? I'm gone a couple of days and you don't recognize my voice?"

"To be perfectly honest, you don't sound like yourself. I mean, now you do, but when you answered the phone, I wasn't sure."

"What's going on?" Evan changed the subject, steering the conversation away from himself.

"Nothing much. Inquiries from a couple of companies that you might think about. Both are in the Far East, looking to expand into the U.S. and European markets. I'll fax you the information so you can look it over, okay?"

"Yeah, sure."

"What about the restaurants? I thought you said there were only a couple of other things that might cause complications. Shouldn't they be wrapped up by now?"

Evan paused for a moment, as he pictured Liz's smile. "It got a little complicated. There are a couple of theme-type restaurants down here which might also work as franchises. Menus vary slightly, but they all target the same crowd. I decided I ought to do a little market research on my own, to make sure we're backing a winner. I can only eat so many times a day," he protested.

"So you're sitting around eating? Has anyone spotted you? Do you think word's gotten out?"

"Not that I'm hiding, but I don't think anyone's recognized me. This isn't the largest account we've ever had, so if people see me, I doubt they'd pick up on what I'm doing because I go to different places every day, sometimes alone, sometimes not. To anyone watching, they'd think it's an ordinary business trip. For that matter, I could be on vacation."

"Evan Delaford never goes on vacation. Period. Anyone who knows your habits would know you are not on vacation. We've worked together what—eight, almost nine years? Ever since you took aim at the big time there's no room in your vocabulary for the term 'personal day'.

"Never mind. I didn't think I'd have to mention it since I figured you'd be back, but there's another reporter doing a story on you and on the success of the company."

Evan groaned. "Not another one. That last 'in depth' profile reporter nearly moved in with me for a month. You have to learn how to get rid of these guys. We don't need any more publicity."

Paul chuckled. "That last reporter was female as I recall. Young and hungry. Not bad looking, either. Of course she wanted to move in with you. Don't they all?

"Not to worry, this one is male, and he's doing one of those lifestyle pieces for *City Life*. So far he's interviewed almost everyone you know, including Aileen. According to her, it sounds like you two will walk down the aisle in the not-too-distant future."

Evan interrupted. "She'll let them think that until she finds another focus for her energy. Or until somebody notices she's not wearing an engagement ring and we haven't seen each other in over a month."

"Who are you dining with?"

"What?"

"You heard me. Who are you eating out with? You mentioned you've found a dining companion."

"Somebody local, who knows the area very well."

"Ah. Let me guess—this local color is female?" surmised Paul.

A vision of Liz at her klutziest, as she appeared last night, crossed Evan's mind. He shook it off.

"Yes. She happens to be a librarian," he answered, hoping to put an end to Paul's incessant questioning.

"Oh." Paul sounded disappointed. He was happily married and wanted to see his friend in the same condition, Evan knew.

Paul had probably conjured up the cliché image of nondescript librarian, Evan supposed. If only he knew how close to the truth he was. "I thought perhaps you met someone."

"I know what you thought. And I did. She's a very interesting woman, who's helping me with my research."

"Interesting . . . as in unattractive?"

"I didn't say that," Evan reminded Paul, not rushing to correct him either. He enjoyed toying with Paul's overactive imagination.

"I suppose she has a great personality, too?"

"As a matter of fact she does," Evan confirmed. *And big green eyes, and great hair, and a figure she's determined to keep a secret . . .*

"You met her at the library?"

"No, we met by accident, in the restaurant in question. She was lunching with her mother," he said, recalling Vivian seated across from him in the booth, insisting he meet her daughter. The entire scenario didn't seem so far-fetched anymore. And Vivian had been right.

"With her mother?" Paul's voice inched up a bit toward the incredulous, obviously picturing Liz as frumpy and gray-haired, complete with ancient mother hobbling along with a walker. "I guess there's no news fodder in *that* story. Evan? Are you there?" Paul spoke loudly into the receiver.

"What?"

"I thought I lost the connection. Keep in mind that there's still a reporter roaming around. Your research assistant, and whoever else you spend time with, might become part of the story. Reporters are constantly searching for new people to interview, you know."

Paul had a valid point. Once these articles started, they seemed to feed on themselves, perpetuating myths from previous pieces which simply weren't true.

"Don't you start believing my press now, Paul. No new scandals or eligible men on the horizon who might catch their attention instead of me? What are they doing? Scraping the dregs since all the good ones got married?"

"Even though Donald Trump *is* back on the market, I think you underestimate yourself, my friend. You are supposedly one of the most fascinating men in the country, or at least in the Midwest, according to any number of magazines. Either that or you've got them all fooled."

"I didn't know I was so interesting."

"Next, you'll be on the cover as the sexiest man alive."

"Yep. That's me—sexy." He looked down at his scabby knees peeking out from beneath the oversized towel wrapped around his waist. *Scabby knees are a must for a sexy man,* he thought. *If they could see me now . . .*

"Aileen has a press agent and gets as much mileage out of the bracelet you gave her as she did holding onto your arm. She works hard to keep the mystery of your relationship alive and in the public eye, you know."

Evan's thoughts drifted. He wondered if he should tell Liz he was one of the sexiest men alive. *Nah,* he thought. *It wouldn't make any difference. She would not be impressed. She'd probably never talk to me again.*

"Why don't you tell the reporters who call that the man they see isn't the real Evan Delaford, he's just a decoy? Tell them the real Evan Delaford is a skinny little nerd who no woman would look at twice." *Boy, isn't that decoy stuff wishful thinking.*

Perhaps, he thought, Liz was onto something. Evan couldn't begin to imagine what it would be like to have his personal life back—to be able to walk into a place without becoming the focus of attention. Maybe if he dressed in old jeans and T-shirts it might help. He'd have to give it a try one of these days.

"Yeah, right. You're a real nerd. According to the stories you're a regular Boy Scout. When you get back, Beverly has a collection for you. She snips everything out of the papers and magazines, since you'd never see this stuff otherwise. You'll get a kick out of it. Evan, we have a deadline on this deal, you know, and with your pushing it back, we'll run close to the wire."

"I knew you were telling me all this other stuff to work in the real question. I should be back in about two weeks."

"Two weeks! You didn't spend two weeks on the Phleger deal, and that was a billion-dollar company. Are you okay?"

"Ouch!" Evan exclaimed, as he bumped one of his injured knees on the corner of the bed. "Yes, I'm fine. I might be back sooner; I'll let you know. Meanwhile, just fax me the new material and I'll start working on it."

"Whatever you say. Oh, I forgot—are you available for centerfolds? Just in case I'm asked?"

"Good-bye, Paul." Evan hung up as Paul chuckled at his own humor.

Two new consulting jobs. Knee abrasions. Centerfolds. Liz Brady. It was a lot for one man to think about.

Chapter Five

The library emptied at the usual time. It was almost quarter to six, and the sky was darkening as the temperature rapidly declined.

Evan Delaford waited in his rental car with the engine off. He considered various approaches, but so far all of them sounded impersonal and hollow. At this rate, he'd never find out why Liz Brady was hiding.

He spent the greater part of the day pursuing the commitment of the local bankers, who were greatly impressed that Evan Delaford himself came to Rockleigh to explore interest in a local operation. It was as if the success of Goodtimes was a salute to their good sense in patronizing the restaurant chain for the past ten years.

At the most awkward moments, however, Liz Brady's vibrant green eyes came to mind, diverting his attention from the business at hand. A very dangerous state of affairs for Evan Delaford. This had never happened before, so it was with natural curiosity that he sat in the car waiting for the woman herself to appear. He wanted to find out what it was about her that kept her on his mind.

Despite the cold, Evan climbed out of the car and leaned against it so he could catch Liz Brady as soon as she emerged from the building.

He recognized her car parked in a space designated for "Head Librarian." No doubt it was an important staff perk. He ran a hand through his hair and glanced at his watch.

Suddenly there she was, walking down the steps and hurrying in the direction of her car.

"Liz!" he called, hoping his voice carried over the wind that whistled through the empty branches of the large oak trees surrounding the parking lot.

She looked up, and a smile spread across her features. After the night before, he thought she might be a bit wary of encountering him in a parking lot!

"Hi, Evan."

He crossed the distance between them, not quite believing the smile on her face. Could it be she was glad to see him? "I thought maybe I missed you. I wasn't sure what your hours were."

The wind whipped sharply around the corner of the building. Strands of Liz's hair blew free of the restraining clip and tumbled down her back and around her face.

She frowned, and the sparkle left her eyes.

"Did you need help with something? For your re-search?" She sounded like an in-charge head librarian. This was going to be a lot harder than he expected.

"Oh no—nothing to do with work. I came to see you," he said, offering no further explanation. Another whoosh of wind rolled a huge pile of leaves from one end of the nearly empty parking lot to the other.

Even though it was freezing, a warm feeling came over Evan. Liz's skirt billowed around her calves and her dark hair flew about her face. He could take her in his arms right now, and smooth those wayward locks. What was it about this woman?

"What did you have in mind?" she asked. "Did you want to try synchronized head bashing again? Maybe there's a heavy metal concert scheduled at the col-lege—we can work out the glitches in our routine."

A grin formed at the side of her mouth as if she couldn't help it. She was amused in spite of herself, he thought.

He responded with a grin of his own, acknowledg-ing the shared experience.

"I only brought a couple of suits with me. I didn't realize I'd signed on for hazardous duty. You know, if the security camera at the restaurant caught our act on film, we could send it to one of those video shows. I'm sure it would win first prize. As it is, I can picture the security personnel reviewing the film from last night. They probably got a big laugh out of it." He chuckled, envisioning the possibility.

"I hope I didn't hurt you too much," she said, eye-ing the top of his head.

"No, it's fine. All those years of childhood spent playing ice hockey should have prepared me for last night's . . . adventure. I'm not usually so . . . uncoordinated. How about you? Are you okay?"

"Yes, I'm fine, despite appearances to the contrary. I did have a headache, but it's better now. Funny you should say uncoordinated, though," she said, a look of puzzlement on her face. "That's exactly the way I've been feeling for the past few months. Perhaps it's contagious."

"Lack of coordination?"

She shrugged, as if confused by her own comment.

"I get in my own way these days. I don't know . . . I was never the most graceful person, but I wasn't an out-and-out klutz. Things like last night happen regularly."

Evan arched a brow. "Did you ever consider the problem might have something to do with the excessive amount of clothing you wear?" he asked.

"What?"

He assessed her coolly from head to toe. "That particular dress has enough fabric to outfit three women and a small child—maybe even an entire village. It might throw off your sense of perspective, kind of like driving a new car and not being sure of how far the front bumper sticks out."

She stared at him like he was out of his mind.

"Does that make any sense to you at all? Because it makes perfect sense to me. I mean, I'm no fashion expert, and women wear things for totally different reasons than men do. But I'm not knocking your dress," he assured her, sensing he dug himself in deeper with each word. He watched her try to figure out what he was talking about.

"Like I said, I'm no fashion expert. I prefer comfortable clothes. Forget I said anything."

"You don't have these conversations very often, do you? With women? About clothes, I mean. And yes, the analogy with the car works. My points of reference aren't what they were before I started wearing such . . . comfortable clothes. But you still haven't told me why you were looking for me."

"Oh," he said, relieved to be let off the hook. He blew out a breath.

"I wanted to thank you," he continued. "For last night. You were a lot of help, you know. As a single diner, it's not feasible to order the amount and range of menu items we did as a couple. I mean, don't you think I'd stand out, if I ordered three appetizers and three entrees?"

"Yes. You'd stand out for sure. I'd wonder how you could eat so much and still look as good as you do. And just for the record, no one has thanked me for cleaning my plate since I was about six years old."

"Thanks . . . I think. That was a compliment, right?"

"Thanks? For which part?"

"The part about me looking as good as I do." Evan's eyes twinkled.

"Oh, well, I just meant, uh, you look pretty good, I mean, like you're in pretty good shape . . ." Liz's words trailed off as if she feared she'd said too much.

"Well, that's encouraging. I wanted to ask you to

go out with me again. No market research, just a simple date. A drink perhaps? Or coffee and dessert?"

Liz stared at him for a moment before answering, an unmistakable look of longing on her face. "I'm sorry Evan, but I don't think so."

"Why not? Have I offended you? Did I do something wrong?"

"No," she said. An awkward pause followed. She took a deep breath before she spoke, not quite looking him in the eye. "It's nothing *you've* said or done, believe me. But after a few rather negative experiences with men, I developed certain rules for myself. I've learned, unfortunately, that if I don't follow my guidelines things end up badly. I enjoy your company. Honestly. Thanks for asking."

What was going on here? Evan wondered. "You're welcome," he said, the wary expression on his face converging the conflicting signals he was receiving. What in the world was this woman talking about? All of a sudden, he remembered something he read in a book review.

"I get it," he said. The overhead light illuminated his face, and the confusion seemed to dissipate all at once. "This is one of those times when we're speaking two different languages—male and female. You enjoy my company. My table manners are acceptable, and my appearance doesn't repulse you. You even paid me a number of compliments. Yet it sounded more like you were enumerating my faults, so you won't be seen with me socially. Right?"

"Oh, no," she said, emphatically shaking her head, "those *were* compliments."

"So? What's the rest of it? There's got to be more. You're declining my invitation, right? Or am I missing something? Are we just not communicating?"

She sighed. "If you must know, it's how you look."

He looked down at himself. No noticeable stains; creases neatly pressed. He hadn't stepped in anything unhygienic. Not even his scabby knees were visible.

"The suit? The tie? My shoes? What?"

Liz shook her head. "No, none of the above."

Evan was genuinely perplexed. "What then?"

"It's you, Evan. You yourself. You're just too good-looking."

"Thank you again, I think. Another backhanded compliment, right? Did your mother teach you this, by any chance?"

Liz remained silent, a somewhat wistful but determined look on her face.

"Can you just explain yourself?"

"It's a long and boring story, I assure you. Let's just say I have a poor track record with guys like you. Trust me."

"What exactly do you mean by 'guys like me'?"

Liz looked uncomfortable. "You know—handsome. Gorgeous. Every woman's dream date."

"You think I'm handsome?" He arched an eyebrow in disbelief.

"Of course."

"Gorgeous?"

"Sure."

"Every woman's dream date?"

"Well, maybe not *every* woman's."

"Certainly not *yours.*"

"It's nothing against you personally."

"No, against my looks, evidently. Like I have control over how I look."

"I'm sorry."

"But that's . . . discrimination!" he exclaimed after a moment. "Are you telling me that if I were homely, you'd go out with me? We could go out on an actual date?"

Liz nodded straight away. "Oh, yes," she said. "Without a doubt. But I can't imagine I'd ever find you unattractive."

He started to laugh, a warm chuckle that gradually built into a full-toothed grin with sound effects.

"Liz, you have no idea, absolutely no idea how wonderful you've made me feel. If only some of my friends could see me now . . . having my so-called good looks get me nowhere with the one woman who genuinely interests me."

He burst into another round of laughter.

Evan didn't notice Liz's look of puzzlement at his reaction, or her half-hearted wave as she drove away.

Evan found a small sports bar crowded mostly with men eating, drinking, and engrossed in the various athletic competitions displayed on multiple television screens. Seated at the bar, he ordered an iced tea and a sandwich and contemplated the evening's televised sporting events.

Liz Brady amazed him. He couldn't say she played hard to get; she obviously meant what she said about not becoming involved with him. He congratulated himself on keeping their initial contact strictly business.

He'd been much too confident of his own appeal. In spite of what her mother told him, Evan was convinced Liz would jump at the chance to go on a date with him. Paul would love this, if he knew. Seeing Evan as the dump-ee instead of the dump-er.

He enjoyed his roast beef with horseradish sauce and mountain-high side of onion rings. A group of die-hard Blackhawks fans alternately roared disappointment and cheered enthusiasm. Next to Evan, a talkative football fan followed another game and expounded on the virtues of the Chicago Bears.

The good food and congenial atmosphere did little to improve his mood. Evan bit into his sandwich and chewed thoughtfully as he watched one of the screens.

What would it take to break through Liz's defenses? He hadn't mistaken the moment of indecision, or the longing in her lovely green eyes. Evan felt sure that those "rules" of hers did nothing but contribute to her internal struggle. She wanted to go out with him, yet she wouldn't let herself. At least, Evan comforted himself, she seemed to feel badly that she couldn't.

He needed a plan to bend those rigid rules of hers so Liz would make a policy change.

If he found the guy responsible for her ridiculous dating code, he was either going to sock him or thank him. After all, if she didn't have regulations to adhere to, Evan knew he'd have a lot more competition for Liz's attention. He'd probably never even have met her!

"Hi, I'm Craig. Are you from out of town?" asked the friendly Bears fan seated on the stool next to him.

"How can you tell?" Evan replied, knowing his tailored suit stood out like a sore thumb among the more casually dressed patrons.

Craig shrugged, his eyes glued to the football game, even though the Bears weren't playing. "Haven't seen you around before."

"I've only been in town for a few days," Evan replied. "This is a great place. Food's not bad either. You come here often?"

"Couple times a week, after work, depending on what games are on. It's the only way I see them all. I don't have cable at the house. They have pools here, you know, during the season. You might like to get in on the action."

While he and Craig discussed sports and the general condition of the construction industry in Rockleigh, Evan absorbed the atmosphere of "The Sports Section."

Most of the patrons appeared to work at manual labor. They were all in pretty good physical shape, except for the occasional beer belly. One thing they all seemed to have in common was grunge. Give any one of them a proper haircut, a shower and a shave, and dress him in a suit and tie, and you'd have what? Somebody just like me, Evan thought. Somebody just like me . . .

A vague plan formed in his mind which might give him some leverage with Liz Brady. He'd have her re-writing that policy and procedures manual of hers so fast it would make her head spin. Miami scored a touchdown, the Blackhawks were in a power play, one of the foreign soccer teams made a goal, and the bar erupted in cheers.

Chapter Six

"**I** knew I'd seen your friend Evan before!" Cindy strode down the main aisle of the library from the research department waving a magazine at Liz. "Just look at this," she said triumphantly, shoving a copy of *Business Journal* into Liz's hands. "He was the June cover story," Cindy went on unnecessarily, since Evan's picture graced the front of the magazine and bold headlines pronounced *"Chicago's Own Donald Trump?"* The question mark at the end didn't detract from the implication.

"Look, look," Cindy said excitedly, grabbing the magazine back from Liz. "There's a whole spread on him in here, his home in Chicago, his life, his *girl-friend.*"

Liz's heart dropped like a stone. There was Evan

Delaford in living color, with a stunning blond draped over his arm.

"She's a former Miss Illinois," Cindy commented. "Your buddy Evan is a real celebrity."

"Yes, I can see," Liz said unenthusiastically. Her initial instincts about Evan were correct after all, she thought as she stared into the smiling eyes of former Miss Illinois. Even though there was a powerful brain behind Evan's male beauty, it appeared Evan wouldn't be seen with anything less than a "ten" on his arm. Compared to Miss Illinois, Liz might rate a "two." Still, Evan *had* asked her out. Why? Comic relief? Temporary entertainment during his stay in Rockleigh? Thank goodness she saved herself the heartache of involvement with him.

Blindly she turned the pages, gazing at shots of Evan's penthouse apartment on Lakeshore Drive, tastefully decorated in "minimalist style." The furnishings were spare and understated, strategically placed in interesting groupings. Even the bedroom was stark, with a wrought iron headboard and bleached oak floors. Liz could have done without the casual shot of Evan stretched out on the satin navy blue comforter, his nose buried in one of Bernard Cornwell's historical novels. He'd probably read the entire series while waiting for Miss Illinois to put on her make-up.

Her composure nearly crumpled as she studied a photo of Evan relaxing in what was described as his den. Surrounded by crammed bookshelves, Evan ruffled the fur of a bright-eyed golden retriever. *He has a dog! And he likes to read,* Liz thought. How much more perfect could a guy get?

Cindy must have noticed Liz's unhappy expression. She touched her arm. "Hey, I thought it was a business thing with you two. Aren't you just friends with this guy?"

Liz forced herself to smile. "Sure. That's what we are—friends." Even to her ears the words sounded unconvincing. "Men and women can just be friends, right?" She closed the magazine and handed it to Cindy, who studied her intently.

"Rarely," Cindy answered. "There's always something going on beneath the surface. And if you're wondering about it, trust me, the attraction's already there." Cindy started back to the reference department, but stopped and turned after a few steps. "I can't blame you for wanting to know what's beneath that particular surface, though. Who wouldn't?"

Liz stuck her tongue out and Cindy walked away, giggling.

The afternoon slowed at the Rockleigh County Library, and Liz found time for one of her favorite activities. Organizing the shelves, replacing books in their appropriate places, checking the rows for misfiles—familiar, comforting tasks. The lump on her head had faded, along with the disquieting possibility of Evan Delaford's pursuit. Even the vague sense of disappointment she felt earlier subsided. The sheltering stacks of the library represented safety. One of the Adopt-a-Shelf volunteers, old Mrs. Shelburn, shuffled along replacing books in the next aisle, and she and Liz traded small talk, even though they were barely visible to each other through the back-to-back book shelves.

A movement at the end of Liz's row distracted her. She glanced up with an automatic smile of greeting and an offer of assistance on her lips. Her expression froze, as the man strolled deliberately toward her. He was tall and broad-shouldered, his hair wavy and un-combed, and a two-day growth of beard covered his face. Liz wondered if her mouth had fallen open as she took in the worn, torn Levi's, faded T-shirt and scuffed sneakers that Evan Delaford wore.

He paused an arm's length away and nearly knocked her off her feet with his killer smile. "Is this more what you had in mind, Miss Brady?" His eyes raked her formless gray jumper and long-sleeved blouse.

Liz bit her lip. Evan's effort to dress down was obviously for her benefit. An attempt, no doubt, to make himself less attractive. It his case, however, it had the reverse effect, making him even more appeal-ing. The dark stubble of beard further emphasized the bright blue of his eyes. Disheveled dark hair brought to mind what he must look like when he awoke in the morning. A snug T-shirt outlined every muscle. Liz snapped her mouth shut in case it hung open without her knowing it.

"What do you think?" Evan prompted. "Am I homely enough now to meet your standards?"

Liz tried very hard not to laugh, but a persistent

smile tugged at the corners of her lips. "I hate to tell you this, but you look even better than you did before." She couldn't help it. The laugh escaped at Evan's crestfallen expression, and before she knew it, she was doubled over trying to smother giggles as tears gathered in her eyes. All the while, Evan leaned against a nearby shelf scowling, arms folded across his chest, waiting for her to finish.

"I'm sorry," she gasped when she was able. "I'm sorry, but you're still—" she grew suddenly serious as his blue eyes snagged hers, "really something," she finished softly.

"So this doesn't work for you?"

"If you're asking do I still find you incredibly attractive—" she glanced away for a moment, "then the answer's yes."

His eyes flickered with interest at her response. "Well, what do you suggest?" he queried as he moved a step closer.

He penned her in, close and tight in the narrow aisle, bookshelves on either side, the wall behind and all of Evan Delaford in front of her. Her gaze wandered from his mussed hair to the soles of his sneakers. She fought the urge to cup his face in her hands just to feel the roughness of his beard.

His gray T-shirt sported a fading athletic logo. Apparently Evan *didn't* spend all his time in pinstriped suits and silk ties. The Levi's, too, had seen their share of wear and tear. They frayed at the pockets and were worn nearly white at the knee. Even the scruffy sneakers didn't detract from Evan's overall appeal. Liz couldn't find one thing wrong with his appearance, and had no idea how somebody like Evan could possibly make himself less appealing.

"Would shaving my head help, do you think?" His voice dropped to a low, intimate tone and he took another step closer.

"I—I don't know," she answered, flustered. "In your case, I doubt it." Turning back to the shelf, she picked up a book and blindly placed it in the row.

Evan stood behind her. "This isn't my fault, you know, the way I look. It's genetic."

Liz nodded, too mesmerized by his presence to speak. This is how it would happen. She'd fall for his pretty face, that hard body moving closer to hers, and then he'd dump her for Miss Ohio or Miss Hawaii the first chance he got. The results would be worse than her experience with Randy, because she might fall for the whole package and not just the exterior.

"You know what I love about you?" he asked softly.

Helplessly, Liz shook her head. Evan hardly knew her. How could he have found something to love about her already?

"You try so hard to restrain this hair of yours," he continued in the same sweet tone, "but all these little wisps and tendrils fight their way free no matter what you do." As though to make his point, he caught one of the offending strands and twirled it around his finger. "Your hair isn't the only thing you're trying to restrain, is it, Liz?" he asked softly.

Like a fool, Liz shook her head again. She was dangerously close to leaning into Evan's arms and letting him hold her forever. *How did he know?* she wondered. *How could he have figured it out when no one else had?* For six months she held back every instinctive feminine urge. She fought dressing to show off her figure, wearing make-up, curling her hair, using perfume, so she would attract the kind of man she needed. Her plan backfired, though, because somehow she attracted Evan Delaford instead. And he was exactly the type of man she *didn't* want.

"Let's forget all this nonsense. Just say you'll go out with me."

His convincing tone almost swayed her. Vaguely, Liz wondered if he used this same tone on his clients to guarantee their agreement to one of his investment deals. The same tone he used on ex-beauty queens, coaxing them into his arms. How many had there been? How long had they lasted? With difficulty, Liz hardened her heart as well as her head against him. She turned to face him, pushing him back a bit with a hand on his chest, fighting for some breathing room. "I'm sorry, Evan, no."

He hooked his thumbs in his pockets and gave her a hard look. "You know what I don't get? You dress down to make yourself less attractive, and that's okay. But when I do it, you still blow me off. I'm sorry I don't have your expertise yet, but with some practice I can probably hide my true self as well as you do."

Surprising her, he stepped closer and wound his index finger once again through a loose strand of hair near her temple. "You know what, Liz? One of these days I'm going to find out exactly what you're hiding under your disguise." He trailed his finger gently along her cheek to her jaw, stopping just beneath her chin. He rubbed the pad of his thumb along her bottom lip, still wearing that determined though puzzled expression. Liz stopped breathing. Surely he intended to kiss her. Abruptly he dropped his hand, and before she realized it, he was gone.

Liz could only be grateful he left when he did. He had totally unnerved her, whether he'd intended to or not. She sank back against the shelf. She had nearly revealed what "lay beneath her disguise" as he put it. A lonely woman seeking a man to love her mind, her heart and her soul. If only she could find a man more interested in brains than beauty. Didn't men know that although jewelry store windows displayed the most eye-catching pieces, the more valuable treasures lay inside?

She could imagine herself falling for Evan Delaford. A brief, blurry fantasy ran through Liz's mind of the two of them holding hands, browsing through bookstores. Next they were honeymooning on a Caribbean island.

She easily envisioned the two of them in his penthouse apartment. Of course, she'd have to redecorate. Liz closed her eyes, imagining the fun she could have adding a woman's touch to Evan's former bachelor pad.

Chapter Seven

"You still haven't found a date for the awards dinner?" Vivian's question sounded casual, but Liz knew the friendly inquiry was fully loaded.

Liz toyed with her pasta, rearranging the slices of chicken, winding noodles around her fork. "No, not yet," she answered.

"But darling, we don't have much time. What are you going to do?"

"I don't know, Mom. Maybe I'll snap my fingers and Mr. Right will materialize from thin air!" Liz knew better than to be so flippant with her mother. There was no place for sarcasm in any conversation with Vivian Brady.

"Darling," Vivian covered Liz's hand with her own. "Please let me help. I know I can find an appropriate escort for you."

"Mom—"

"Now what about your cousin, Lenny?"

"Lenny weighs three hundred pounds, Mom. I don't think they rent tuxedos in his size."

"Hmmm. Yes, you're probably right." Vivian appeared to ponder the problem for a moment while she nibbled on a slice of garlic bread.

"I know!" She snapped her fingers as though a brilliant idea just occurred to her. "What about that nice young man you met at the church social last spring. Andrew? Aaron? What was his name?"

"Arthur McPherson?" Liz responded.

"Yes, that's it. He seemed like a lovely young man. I never did understand why you only went out with him once. He called and called, remember? And you wouldn't give him the time of day."

"His wife might have had something to do with that, Mom, don't you remember? Arthur failed to mention he was married before I agreed to go out with him. Mrs. McPherson followed us on our date, made a scene in the restaurant and dumped a pitcher of iced tea on Arthur's head. I had to call you to come pick me up," Liz reminded Vivian.

"Oh my, yes, that's right. I'd forgotten. He really was a darling man. Too bad he was already married."

"Hello, Liz. Mrs. Brady." Liz glanced up as the owner of the feminine voice stopped at their table amid a cloud of heavy perfume.

Liz forced a phony smile for the visitor. "Hello, Caroline. How are you?"

Caroline Winters-Spellman was the most deeply insecure woman Liz had ever met. She made a career of picking apart any female who could possibly represent a challenge to her. Liz had endured her share of Caroline's barbs during their years at Rockleigh High. Not even her subsequent marriage to Ralph Spellman—who was now mayor of Rockleigh—improved Caroline's view of the world and her place in it. Over the years she honed her ability to spot an opponent's most vulnerable area, and developed an unerring instinct for zeroing in on it with minimal effort. Liz braced herself as Caroline's vulture-like gaze traveled over her as if she were trying to decide where to start.

"I'm just fine, Liz. It's *you* I'm worried about. Sandy Burns mentioned she'd seen you in the library recently, and you looked decidedly unwell. My goodness, she was right! I hope it's nothing serious."

"I assure you, Caroline, I'm in perfect health." Liz's jaw clenched but she kept her smile in place.

"Oh, but you're terribly pale! Don't you think so, Mrs. Brady?"

"No more so than usual," Vivian commented. Was her mother enjoying this, Liz wondered, having the vicious Caroline concur with her on her daughter's appearance?

"Maybe it's the colors you're wearing," Caroline offered. "Certain shades of brown and gray, do tend to drain the color from one's complexion," she said authoritatively. "That is, assuming one has some color to begin with.

"Well, it's none of my business," Caroline laughed,

completely oblivious to Liz's stony silence. "Though I do have the name of a style consultant in St. Louis. She's done wonders for a couple of people I know. She might even be able to help you, Liz." Caroline's tone implied she thought this highly unlikely. "Well, I must run. Liz, if you won't see a doctor you might want to give Roger over at Chez Hair a call. I understand they're running a special on makeovers next month."

"Good-bye, Caroline," Liz returned sweetly.

"Bye, now. Bye-bye, Mrs. Brady." Caroline swept out, her boyish hips swaying beneath the skirt of her designer suit.

"Witch," Liz muttered under her breath as she glared at Caroline's retreating form.

"Caroline seems to be doing very well for herself," Vivian commented. "I understand Ralph took her to Europe over the summer."

"Too bad he brought her back, isn't it?"

"She's always so beautifully dressed. I wonder where she shops," Vivian said absently. "Her hair looks good with those highlights, too. She probably spends a fortune at the salon. Do you suppose she has her nails done at Chez Hair?"

Liz rolled her eyes in resignation. "I'm sure I wouldn't know, Mother. Mom? Hello?" Somehow when something or someone served Vivian's purposes, she managed to completely zone out.

"Of course, she's always been a tad critical of you, dear," Vivian said as her focus shifted back to the present. She eyed her daughter across the table. "Though perhaps not without reason."

"Could we please talk about something else? I'm losing my appetite."

"Of course, dear. Now where were we? Oh, I know! Maybe you could ask that fellow, that new friend of yours you met in Goodtimes last week. He sounded nice. Too bad I missed him. Well, you know my motto—when opportunity knocks, I'm always in the ladies' room. Have you heard from him since your dinner the other night?"

Liz had known the moment she mentioned Evan Delaford to her mother she was going to regret it. Vivian never missed an opportunity to ask whether Liz had seen him, and managed to glean every detail of their few encounters.

"No, Mom. That's strictly business. I can't date him." *Liar,* Liz told herself. After yesterday's encounter, *I can't stop thinking about him.*

"Oh, that's too bad, dear. I bet he'd be perfect. He sounds like the kind of man who comes with his own tux."

"Yes, he probably does." The opportunity to agree with her mother about men happened so rarely Liz felt obligated to take advantage of each one.

"You did him a favor by having dinner with him, didn't you say? Maybe he could return it by being your escort for the banquet."

Evan was the last person Liz wanted to discuss with her mother; she was confused enough. "Mom, stop worrying about this, okay? I'll find a date."

Vivian sat back in her chair and regarded Liz across the table. "How? By dressing like a senior citizen? Burying yourself in that library from dawn 'til dusk? Liz, you are beautiful inside, and I certainly know how smart you are. But Caroline was right. You're crazy if you expect a man to get a glimpse of that brain of yours without hanging out a sign. A restaurant might serve gourmet food, but if it looks like a dump, who'll give it a try?"

"Someone who looks beyond the outward appearance of the place?" Liz asked. "Someone who's adventurous, not afraid to try something different?" How dare her mother take Caroline's side!

"Huh. Well, if you think it'll be a man, think again. With men, it pays to advertise. And the bigger and better the sign, the more successful you'll be."

"Yeah, Mom, I know," Liz agreed. Vivian failed to grasp the problem. Liz didn't *want* a man who saw the sign and came looking for more. She wanted one who could look beyond the façade and be fascinated by what he found underneath. Somebody like Evan, perhaps? As quickly as the thought popped into her head she pushed it away.

"Sweetheart, you need a date. Let me set something up for you, just this once. I know this will work if you just give it a try. Please? I don't want you to be alone at the dinner."

Shielding herself against Caroline's well-placed arrows had worn Liz down. She was exhausted by the prospect of arguing further with her mother. What was the harm in allowing Vivian the one opportunity to do what she herself could not? "Okay, Mom. Go ahead. You can't do any worse than I have."

"Hi."

Liz turned abruptly from the shelves where she was rearranging encyclopedia volumes to make room for new reference materials. "Hi," she answered, hating the way her heart pounded faster just because he stood so close.

Evan was still dressed down, although today he wore a blue polo shirt that matched his eyes and a pair of khakis. Perhaps he had run a brush through his hair earlier, but he hadn't bothered to shave. The increased growth of beard made him look sexy and dangerous.

After her mother's comments, Liz had applied lipstick before returning to the library. Not that anyone would notice.

"Look, I want to apologize for yesterday," Evan said.

"There's no need—"

"Yes, there is," Even interrupted her. "If you don't want to go out with me, it doesn't matter what your reasons are. As my father used to say, somebody can dislike you because of the way you part your hair."

"It's not your hair—" Liz tried again.

"Whatever." He waved away her interruption. "I should just accept you're not interested and leave it alone."

Liz swallowed. Was this what she wanted him to do? In spite of all the reasons she'd given herself not to be, she *was* interested.

"The thing is," Evan went on, "I enjoy your company. And you *did* say you'd help me with my research, remember?"

Liz nodded, fascinated by the way Evan's lips moved when he spoke. Her gaze traveled over his shadowed jaw and up to his bright blue eyes, barely hearing his words.

"So I wondered if you'd still have dinner with me."

Liz nodded again. She'd agree to just about anything, if he'd keep talking to her in that seductive tone. If he'd let her look at him and not mind that she couldn't seem to concentrate on anything except his mouth.

"Strictly business, of course," Evan added, moving a couple of inches closer to her.

"Sure," Liz said. "Strictly business."

His fingertips brushed her collarbone, sending tingles down her spine. She launched herself at him at the same time as he yanked her forward. She wound her arms around his neck. All she wanted was a kiss. Just one kiss.

Her hair came loose. Her feet left the ground as he hugged her against him, backing her up against the shelf behind her.

At some level Liz felt the books digging into her flesh, but the sensation was insignificant. This was what she needed, a man who erased all rational thought with a simple kiss. A man who literally swept her off her feet. A man who took her out of place and time and forced her to concentrate on nothing but him. Who cared what he looked like?

A thumping noise slowly got Liz's attention. A thwack. A thud. Another thwack, then another, then another. Eventually she tore herself away from Evan to figure out what exactly had caused that sound. It sounded like books falling to the floor, but as long as she was in Evan's arms, it didn't really matter where the noise came from. Or did it?

Evan suddenly broke the kiss. She glanced up, but his attention was focused over her shoulder. Following his gaze, she understood why.

Several teenagers from the tutoring session gaped at them from the young adult section. Liz chanced a brief glance to the floor behind her, not terribly surprised to see an entire set of encyclopedias laying in disarray.

Her gaze flew back to Evan's as he slowly released her, allowing her feet to touch the floor again. She turned back to the now-giggling group of kids, noting the shocked expression of their teacher, Mrs. Headley. "Uh, sorry about that. We were just—uh, rearranging a few things over here." Mrs. Headley telegraphed her disapproval with an arched brow and a harrumph of displeasure at the interruption. "Sorry," Liz offered again with a guilty cringe, and led Evan toward the end of the aisle.

"Pick you up around seven?" His blue eyes danced at Liz's discomfiture. He ran his fingers gently through her mussed hair.

"I'm not so sure now," Liz answered him shakily.

"Uh-uh. You promised. Strictly business, remember?"

He smiled and dropped his hands. Rubbing a thumb against the corner of her mouth, he whispered, "Nice lipstick," and then he was gone.

Chapter Eight

Evan *noticed my lipstick,* Liz thought during the rest of the dream-like afternoon. Perhaps it was time to give him a little test, and see what else he noticed.

Liz arrived home and promptly began preparing for her "business" dinner with Evan Delaford. She'd keep it subtle, she decided as she slid into a tub full of perfume-scented bubbles. It wouldn't pay to show all her cards at once. Not with a man like Evan Delaford.

For the first time in many months, Liz eyed her wardrobe critically. She needed a dressy outfit, but not too different from her current style. She pulled a long-sleeved cowl neck knit dress from the depths of her closet. The bodice draped attractively across the bust-line and the full skirt fell to just below the knee.

Shoes. Not the flats she normally wore. Wistfully she fingered a strappy black pair with a high heel. Not

72

quite right. She settled on a perfectly acceptable pair of patent leather pumps with a one-inch heel.

Now then, what about her hair? She couldn't leave it down the way Evan saw her last. Otherwise he'd have no reason to dream about pulling it loose again. She giggled at her reflection as she slicked back the wayward strands he seemed so fond of with an extra dose of gel.

Make-up? A bit of powder, a touch of mascara, and since Evan seemed to like lipstick, she took extra time with her mouth.

With her glasses in place, Liz stepped back to review her work in the full-length mirror. The mauve dress emphasized her curves more than she liked, but after today Evan had a pretty good idea of what she'd been hiding anyway. She hoped she wasn't showing too much calf.

Liz twisted and turned, admiring the slick, neat knot of hair at the back of her head and the way the dress hugged her waistline. Even her eyes sparkled behind the lenses of her glasses. *Perfect,* she thought. *I look like a cross between my fifth-grade teacher and a Sports Illustrated swimsuit cover model.*

Business or pleasure? Evan wouldn't know which way to play it. She congratulated herself as she added a pair of tiny jet earrings to the ensemble. Maybe he'd be as confused about what was developing between them as she was.

Liz's certainty that she had thrown Evan off-balance eroded steadily during the evening. He hid his initial shock at her appearance well, and commented only that she looked nice. He made a concerted effort to maintain the business-like relationship he proposed earlier. His steady blue gaze admired her throughout the meal, unsettling her.

Liz was so rattled by the vibes between them she barely tasted her food. She made up imaginative responses to Evan's questions about each dish, drawing on her memory of culinary terms.

"There's a hint of fennel in the soup. It's wonderful."

"I'd like a bit more endive in the salad, and they overdid the garlic in the croutons."

"The salad dressing?" She paused for effect, tasting a tiny bit of the Italian blend from the end of her pinky finger. "The use of extra virgin olive oil would be an improvement, I think, and it's a bit heavy on the oregano."

By the time her chicken Florentine arrived, she had nearly run out of such comments and was close to telling Evan the truth: she could barely taste the food because she was with him. Her mind was distracted, her insides were mush. The thought of more than friendship with him drove her to distraction. Somehow she managed to hang on until the end of the meal.

"There's too much spinach in it," was her only comment when Evan asked about her entree.

"That was pleasant," she said from the passenger seat as they pulled out of the parking lot. Was there any point in either of them continuing this charade?

"Hmmm," Evan agreed non-committally with a glance in her direction.

"I like your car." Liz stretched against the leather upholstery like a cat. She kicked off her shoes and buried her toes in the luxurious carpeting. Without thinking, she released the clip holding her hair in place and shook it out, letting it fall to her shoulders. "Oh, this is great."

She crossed her legs, subtly rearranging her skirt to show just a bit of knee, pretending not to notice when Evan took his eyes off the road to study her legs. *It is pretty dark out anyway,* she reminded herself, *except for the streetlights. He's not able to see much.* Neither would she once she slipped her glasses off, but she stowed them in her purse, hoping she wouldn't need them for the rest of the evening.

She ran her fingers along the console between them. "What kind of car is this? A Cadillac?"

Evan watched her every move. His hands tightened on the steering wheel. "Seville," he replied, clearing his throat. He shifted in his seat and ran a finger around the collar of his shirt.

"Hmmm," Liz murmured, "Maybe you'd let me drive it sometime?"

Evan yanked his gaze from the console back to the road and accelerated, racing through a red light. "Any time, Liz. I'm sure you'd enjoy the way it handles."

"Smooth, I bet."

"Yes. Very smooth."

"It's not hard to control, is it?" she inquired.

"It can be." He braked to a halt in front of Liz's

house. He had his seatbelt off in a flash and in one deft movement he brought her hand to his lips. He placed a hot kiss on her palm before reaching for her.

His lips seared hers. A fireworks display went off behind her closed eyelids. Flashing red and blue lights, a dizzying spectrum of feelings washed over her as Evan pulled her closer.

Time was forgotten as they concentrated on getting to know each other better. When was the last time she felt this kind of excitement? High school, probably.

She brushed the back of her hand along Evan's once again smooth-shaven jaw, and buried her fingers in the wavy hair at his nape.

There was a loud knock on the car window. It took what seemed like a very long time to open her eyes, separate her lips from Evan's, and still she saw fireworks. Or what she assumed were fireworks.

"Step out of the vehicle, please." This command was issued in a stern male voice from just beyond the car window.

Liz blinked again and it suddenly occurred to her that the blurry fireworks were actually the flashing lights of the police car parked behind them. Her confused gaze met Evan's.

"Busted," he whispered, as a bright light glared through the window, nearly blinding them both.

"Police! Step out of the vehicle, *now!*" roared the voice on the other side.

Evan released the lock, but before he could open the door it was yanked open and Liz tumbled out into the arms of the police officer on the other side. In a split second Evan stood next to her, steadying her while the cop looked them over. "All right, folks, let's see some ID."

"What's this all about, officer?" Evan asked as he reached for his wallet.

"Nice and easy there, fella," the cop warned as Evan withdrew his wallet from his back pocket. Handing his license to the officer, he ducked back into the car for Liz's purse.

The cop had finished looking over the license by the time Evan handed Liz her purse. "Registration for the vehicle, sir?" he asked politely as Liz handed him her license.

While Evan scoured the rental car's glove compartment for the registration, the police officer looked over Liz's driver's license. "Elizabeth Brady," he murmured. His head came up and he gazed at Liz in puzzlement in the combined light of the squad car, the Cadillac and the flashlight.

"Liz?" he gasped. "Liz Brady?"

Liz, squinted at the policeman for a moment, trying to bring him into clearer focus before a huge smile spread across her face. "Joey? Joey Patrillo?"

He nodded and Liz pounced on him in delight. He gathered her into a bear hug, both oblivious to a perturbed Evan, who closed the car door and stood, registration in hand.

"Joey Patrillo! I don't believe it!" Liz exclaimed. "You're a cop?"

"Have been for seven years," Officer Patrillo proclaimed proudly. "You'd know that if you'd shown up at our ten-year class reunion."

"I know," Liz agreed. "But my dad passed away right around then. I just wasn't up for it."

"Aw, I'm sorry," Joey offered. "It's great to see you, Liz." He glanced in Evan's direction.

"Oh, I'm sorry. Evan Delaford, Joey—uh—Joe Patrillo. Joey and I dated in high school," she added by way of explanation.

Evan grunted an acknowledgment and took the hand Officer Patrillo offered. Joey doffed his cap and Liz knew Officer Patrillo with his black wavy hair and dark eyes would be considered quite handsome by the average woman. Liz didn't miss the appraising look Evan gave the other man.

Joey turned his attention back to Liz. "This sure brings back some memories, huh? Remember my old man's Ford LTD with the big back seat? A whole gang of us used to head up to the lake and—"

Evan cleared his throat loudly, meaningfully, bringing Joey's trip down memory lane to an abrupt close. He took the registration from Evan but barely glanced at it. "You two just arriving home for the evening?" he inquired, his gaze raking over Evan before returning to Liz.

"Uh, yes, we were—" Liz somehow felt trapped between the two men. "Just saying good-night," she finished in a massive understatement.

Joey's eyes again returned to Evan, who remained passively silent as though he had no need to defend his actions. Joey addressed the rest of his comments to Liz. "We've had reports of prowlers in the neighborhood," he informed her. "A couple of attempted break-ins. Probably kids, but be careful, okay?"

"I will, Joey. Thanks." Liz smiled at him.

"Good to see you again, Liz." He nodded at Evan. "Sorry for the interruption."

The way he said it, even Liz knew Joey had no regrets. They both watched as Joey returned to his patrol car, turned off the flashing lights and saluted as he drove off.

Liz felt ridiculously light-hearted as she walked to the door. Evan followed, almost somberly. Liz was sure she'd seen a flash of jealousy in Evan's eyes when Joey had mentioned their shared history. She, for one, was grateful for the interruption. It seemed there was a thin, easily crossed line between business and pleasure.

At her door, she turned to him and offered her hand. This was supposed to be strictly business, after all. If the gesture surprised him, Evan didn't show it. Instead he took her hand and held it in his larger one. So much for keeping him at arm's length, Liz told herself. He didn't have to kiss her; all he had to do was touch her and she tingled inside. For several seconds she waited to see if he would do more or say something, but when he did, it was not what she expected. He brought her hand to his lips and kissed it as though she were a princess, and he a knight seeking her favor.

His blue eyes had a devilish glint, caused either by his own thoughts or the play of porchlight. Reaching behind her, he pushed open the door she had just unlocked. "Good night, Liz."

Chapter Nine

Liz drummed her fingers on the table in irritation, and gazed out the window. She had been in Goodtimes so often the past week she had practically memorized the menu. Still, it was a convenient place to meet the man her mother insisted would be perfect for her, based on her now newly acquired expertise in perusing the personal ads.

Liz had her doubts about the "Are you the right one for me?" drivel, but she admitted the rest of it sounded pretty good. "Looking for a special relationship with a special woman . . . If you want to be taken care of by a good man . . . serious inquiries only need reply."

A tiny blue sports car swerved into a parking place directly in Liz's line of vision. She smiled as she watched the male driver tousle his professionally high-lighted locks in the rearview mirror, arranging them over his forehead. She nearly laughed out loud as he squirted breath spray into his mouth exactly twice before exiting the vehicle. Giving the car a loving pat, he crossed to the door. *Wow,* Liz thought, *this guy must have some big plans for the afternoon.* He wore white jeans which hugged muscle-bound thighs, and a dark blue polo shirt that exactly matched the shade of his car. *Okay to stare at a good-looking guy,* she reminded herself. *You just don't go out with him.*

Absently swirling the straw in her iced tea, Liz glanced at her watch. Her "date" was ten minutes late.

"Hi, um . . ."

Liz looked up to see Mr. Blue Sports Car next to her table, shuffling through the pages of a tiny notebook.

"Liz?" he questioned.

She nodded, hating herself for doing so. Was this the dream date her mother chose? Why, oh, why hadn't she said, no, sorry my name is Sally, or Lucy, or Princess Stephanie? Why did she admit to being Liz?

"Hi. I'm Kenny." He flashed a bright smile and Liz swallowed as he slid into the seat across from her. He would never do. For one thing, if this guy was anywhere near thirty she'd be shocked. He didn't look a day over twenty-two.

"So you liked my ad, huh?" Kenny said as he opened the menu.

"It was . . . intriguing," Liz answered cautiously, wondering if Kenny even knew what the word meant.

"Intriguing, yeah. I like that. It means like you're

intrigued, right? You're not the only one," he told her reassuringly.

"Really?" Liz raised an eyebrow as though fascinated.

"Oh, yeah!" He gazed at her with boyish enthusiasm. "I never knew there were so many desperate lonely women out there. They'll do anything just to get a da—," he stalled. "Just to meet a nice guy," he amended.

"See, the trick is, with those ads, you gotta make it sound like you're only concerned with what the ladies want. It's not good if you say too much about yourself at first."

This from an expert at writing personal ads. "I see," Liz said. "I suppose most of the women who respond are older than you?"

"Well, yeah, mostly. But girls my age are not as willing to—"

"Fall for your pickup lines?" Liz smiled. *Thank you, Mom. This guy is perfect.*

Kenny didn't answer. Something else snagged his attention. Liz swung her gaze in the same direction. All she could see was Tiffany, the cute waitress from the other night juggling a handful of silverware while setting an empty table nearby. Was Kenny interested in the waitress, or was he just easily distracted by shiny objects? Liz sighed. Should she cut her losses immediately, or stay and at least get something to eat? She could hear Vivian now: *You didn't give him a chance. What can you tell after five minutes with a man?*

Liz looked at the man across the table. He's too young, too vapid, too muscle-bound. Besides that, she was willing to bet his immediate goals in life were to have his highlighted hair touched up before the end of the week and to add another two inches to his biceps by year-end. Thanks, Mom. Thanks a lot.

Liz's mind was made up when the cute waitress came to take their order. By the time Kenny took his attention away from Tiffany and placed his order for "angle" hair pasta instead of angel hair, she vowed to survive lunch, get through the afternoon and stop by to kill her mother on the way home. Even Tiffany winced and offered Liz a sympathetic look as Kenny's mispronunciation brought images of geometrically shaped noodles to mind.

Thinking she could always report back to Evan if she saw him again, Liz ordered the quesadillas, which she'd never had before.

After Tiffany left, Kenny continued to study the menu, his brow furrowed intently. "I don't see what you ordered on here." He shot her a puzzled look.

"It's right there." Liz tapped the menu.

"Kwes-a-dill-as?" he sounded out painfully. "That's not what you said, is it?"

"Kase-a-dee-as. It's Spanish. It's not pronounced like it's spelled. A lot of things aren't."

Her rebuke went over his head and he brightened. Picking up his glass of milk, he saluted her before downing half of it in a huge gulp.

Evan Delaford chose that moment to make an appearance. "Hello, Liz."

All at once he was there, gazing down at her with interest. His gaze moved to Kenny, a question in his eyes. Liz frowned and fought the urge to wipe Kenny's milk mustache from his lip before she introduced them. "Hi, Evan. This is my . . . friend, Kenny." *Did Kenny have a last name?* Liz wondered. *More importantly, did he know what it was?* Perhaps it was difficult to pronounce and he feared being asked to spell it.

"Hey, how's it going?" Kenny nodded up at Evan before his attention was snared by the jangling bracelets of the woman at the table across from them.

Evan made no move to leave. Just as he opened his mouth to speak, Kenny's concentration reasserted itself. "You work out? You look like you're in pretty good shape." He looked Evan up and down, perusing with interest the broad shoulders and long legs. Oh great, Liz thought. Nowhere in Kenny's ad had it stated only women need apply.

Evan shrugged in answer to Kenny's question. "Not regularly. Couple times a week if I'm lucky. Racquetball when I can."

"Hang on, I'll give you my card. I'm a personal trainer." Kenny struggled to dislodge his wallet from the back pocket of his too-tight jeans, using the table for leverage. The wallet came loose too quickly and threw him off-balance. The table tipped and sent his half glass of milk and Liz's iced tea into her lap.

Liz shrieked as Evan stepped back to avoid the splash. Her cheeks flamed. "Oh! Oh!" Liz sputtered as she stood and tried to dab at the mess on her skirt.

Evan quickly snatched a dry napkin from another table to assist. The breath caught in her throat as his hand held hers while he dabbed at her damp sleeve. "Better?" Liz could barely stammer a response as her knees threatened to buckle. With her own napkin she brushed ineffectually at her sopping skirt.

"Sorry . . . uh . . ." This came from Kenny, who had been momentarily forgotten. The apology was directed at Liz, but it was ruined when he opened his mouth to continue. "What was your name again?"

Liz wished the floor would open up and swallow her whole so she wouldn't have to witness Evan's smirk. He accepted the business card Kenny pushed toward him. "Is he toilet-trained, yet?" Evan asked in an audible whisper before a huge grin spread across his face and he took off.

Without a word to the somewhat confused Kenny, Liz made a beeline for the restroom. She cleaned up as best she could, and looked in the mirror and sighed. Evan was probably outside waiting to pounce on her for an explanation. How could she admit to Evan of all people that she was so desperate for a date that she'd allowed her mother to fix her up through a personal ad? She couldn't believe she'd agreed to such a thing. She'd broken the biggest rule in her rulebook.

If nothing else, her disastrous luncheon with Kenny confirmed that Liz's instincts were right. Her policy to stay away from any man her mother arranged for her to meet would remain firmly intact.

* * *

"I think you've got some 'splaining to do, Lucy." Evan did his best Ricky Ricardo imitation as he fell into step beside Liz. Surely she didn't think she could get off that easily, slip through the restaurant and get to her car without some kind of explanation.

She glanced up at him, her chin lifted defiantly. "I don't know what you're talking about."

"I'm sure you do, but just in case, I'll clarify. You don't date good-looking men, remember?" He had to give her credit. Even with her damp clothes and the fiasco of just a few minutes ago, she regained her composure and had no trouble meeting his eyes.

"That's right, I don't," she agreed.

"So what was going on in there with your friend Kenny? Business or pleasure?"

"Neither, actually." Was it his imagination, or did Liz repress a shudder at the mention of Kenny? "He's—he's a friend of my mother's."

"Yeah, right." Evan wasn't buying that for a minute. He also wasn't going to budge until Liz came clean with him.

"All right! My mother fixed me up with him."

"Why would she do that? She knows you don't date guys like him."

Liz's eyes flashed with suspicion. "How do you know what my mother thinks about anything?"

Evan thought quickly to cover his blunder. "I just— I assumed she'd know your preferences in men, and choose someone more . . . appropriate, that's all." Someone like me, he wanted to add, but didn't.

Liz folded her arms across her chest and stuck out

her lower lip. "Yes, well, it doesn't matter. I wouldn't go out with him anyway."

"Why?" Evan asked, trying not to smile at her defensive posture and little-girl pout. "Because he's too good-looking?"

Liz's gaze met his. She shrugged. "I might be able to overlook that, but—"

"But what?" Evan pushed.

"My mother set me up with Kenny."

The light began to dawn, or so Evan thought. "And you knew nothing about it."

"No, I agreed to it."

Evan's mouth opened in surprise. "Huh? So you'll date good-looking guys as long as they're airheads?"

"No!"

"You won't date them at all?"

"Yes!"

"You will or you won't?"

"Right."

Evan's mind whirled in confusion. "But you just said you knew your mother set you up with Kenny."

"Yes, but I didn't know he was good-looking."

"But you did know he was an air-head?"

"No."

That cleared up nothing. "So you won't go out with him?"

"No, I won't."

Now they were getting somewhere.

"Because he's good-looking?"

"No, that's not it."

"Because he's an air-head?"

"No, not just because of that, either."

"Then why?" Evan nearly shouted in frustration. And why was he so concerned whether she'd go out with another man? All he really wanted to do was to figure out how to get her to go out with *him!*

"Because my mother set it up," Liz explained as though she were talking to a three-year-old.

"But—but—" Evan was speechless. Liz's conflicting dating policies were about as easy to fathom as the political ones of the current White House administration.

"I made an exception today, but I shouldn't have, and if nothing else, I know that now. No way would I ever date a man my mother set me up with." She paused for a moment. "You should understand."

"I should?" In truth, Evan felt as though he'd just been kicked in the gut. Or maybe in the head. He understood nothing.

"After the disaster you witnessed today, it should be crystal clear. I have to get back to work."

Evan's problems seemed to compound by the minute. Not only did he have to figure out how to convince Liz to date him, he also needed to find a way to confess that if not for her mother, he might never have met her.

"Liz, wait." He touched her arm as she opened her car door, delaying her departure. Sensing his timing was dreadfully off, he plunged ahead anyway. "Have dinner with me tonight." As if he knew she planned to refuse he waited just a beat before adding a heartfelt, "Please."

Liz shook her head anyway. "I can't. Not tonight, anyway."

Evan didn't even try to hide his disappointment. Or his determination. "Tomorrow then?"

Liz gave him a saucy smile, even though she was far from light-hearted at the moment. "Maybe."

If Liz had suffered even a pang of regret over refusing Evan's dinner invitation, it disappeared as soon as the doorbell announced the arrival of her piping hot garlic-crust pizza with the works. She had a deal with Richie Camden, the delivery boy. She left the money for the pizza plus his generous tip in an envelope outside the front door, and he left the pizza without waiting for her to answer the bell.

Tonight was her night to pamper herself. Nothing and no one interfered with her monthly ritual—not even Evan Delaford. She might not be on a rampage to attract a man, but that didn't mean she didn't take care of herself. Besides, pampering herself was a surefire way to make herself feel better after the disastrous day she'd had. She'd soaked in an aromatherapy bath for nearly forty-five minutes and was now comfortably wrapped in her ancient terry cloth robe. After applying a hot oil treatment to her hair, she carefully wound plastic wrap around her scalp as directed. Next came the application of a deep-pore cleansing mask in an oh-so-attractive shade of muddy green. She slathered the mask on, along with a generous dollop of depilatory over her upper lip before proceeding to the pedicure portion of the evening. She finished the topcoat of candy apple red, and with the foam separators stuck between her toes, waddled to the front door. She remembered not to lick her lips at the thought of devouring an entire pizza by herself, one of her must-reads on her lap and a cold glass of orange soda nearby. Ah! The perfect evening.

She swung the door wide open and bent to scoop up the pizza as a pair of feet came to a stop on the other side of the box. A thief about to abscond with her pizza! When she grabbed for the pizza and attempted to straighten quickly, the top of her head made contact with the visitor's chin.

"Yeow!" He stepped back, rubbing his chin with his fingers, as Liz stood up with a firm grasp on the pizza box. "You are one lethal lady," Evan told her, eyeing her as though waiting for the next surprise move.

"Evan!" Liz didn't have to fake her surprise.

"Working on your Halloween costume, I see. That's quite a disguise. What are you going as? The Creature from the Black Lagoon?"

"Oh no! Oh, Evan, what are you doing here?" Liz cried as she suddenly remembered her appearance.

"You know me. Can't go more than a week without a blow to the head."

Liz didn't know whether to run and hide or invite him in. Should she stand there in the doorway in this get-up, gaping at him while the entire neighborhood looked on? As she contemplated her options, a dribble of hot oil escaped the plastic wrap and ran down her temple to her cheek. *I'm melting, I'm melting,* she thought. At the moment she could certainly give the Wicked Witch of the West a run for her money.

"I understand you try to play down your attractiveness, Liz, but I think you've gone too far. You need help," said Evan, who was still rubbing his chin and staring at her bug-eyed.

Her clay mask was starting to crack, and Evan Delaford was expounding on her need for psychotherapy. Maybe she was nuts, because she was going to invite him in. She stepped back, indicating he should follow her inside. She turned to close the door, and the foam pads between her toes became entwined in a loose strand of the colorful rag rug on which she stood.

Wildly, she attempted to save the pizza as she lost her footing. Evan made a grab for it, managing to wrest the box from her just as she pitched forward against him. They went down together. A loud rushing whoosh of air expelled from Evan's lungs. Liz landed on top of him, the rag rug still entangled between her toes, the pizza box hopelessly smashed between them. It took her a moment to regain her senses as she looked down into Evan's to-die-for blue eyes while he caught his breath. "You are definitely a dangerous woman," he informed her.

In spite of herself, Liz smiled. Without thinking, she lowered her head toward Evan's. He braced her firmly above him with both hands on her upper arms. *What's wrong with him?* she wondered. *He had certainly wanted to kiss me last night.* At that moment a blob of hot oil mixed with clay mask dropped onto Evan's cheek. While Liz studied it, a tiny glob of depilatory landed on his nose. "You're dripping," Evan pointed out.

"Oh!" Liz jumped off Evan and righted herself, clutching her robe around her. Evan was wrong—she wasn't the one who was dangerous. He was. Being close to him made her lose all rational thought. Time and place and circumstance flitted through her scrambled brain like water passing through a sieve. It was definitely time for a reality check.

Evan set the ruined pizza aside and hauled himself up off the floor. Were all of their meetings destined to be like this? With one or the other of them landing on a horizontal surface due to an incident which inevitably involved damaged clothing?

It was hard to say who was more of a disaster at the moment—Liz or Evan. True, hot oil treatment, facial mask and depilatory were running down her neck and dripping all over her robe, but Evan bore evidence of all of these substances along with a large grease stain and traces of tomato sauce on his previously spotless shirt. "I ruined your pizza," he told her apologetically, handing the smashed and leaking box to her.

"We could order another one."

"We?"

"Unless you've already eaten," Liz amended.

Evan relaxed a notch. "No, as a matter of fact. I stopped by to see if I could persuade you to change your mind about having dinner with me."

At least that explained why he'd appeared on her doorstep. Liz pointed Evan in the direction of the bathroom next to the second bedroom to clean up while she dashed into her room. She quickly ordered another pizza and jumped in the shower. Richie would know something was up, but she tipped him enough not to ask questions.

She yanked on an ancient pair of gray sweats and didn't take time to blow dry her hair.

A half hour later she and Evan sat across from each other sharing a large pizza.

A new Evan, Liz thought to herself, *dressed down but clean-shaven. Still a hunk, but that wasn't likely to change no matter what he wore.*

She studied him as they talked of everything and nothing. Books they'd read, their respective college careers, even the difference in the weather patterns between Chicago and Rockleigh. *It's too bad,* Liz thought sadly. *He had all those gorgeous women lined up, just waiting for him to glance their way.* And now he'd seen her at her absolute worst, something she'd hidden from every other man she'd ever dated. But maybe that was a good thing. If Evan pursued her after this, she would finally have proven her point.

Chapter Ten

The following afternoon, Liz decided she needed a break. Desperately. She'd stockpiled her vacation time all year, though to what end she didn't know. Perhaps she'd suggest a singles cruise to her mother after all. At any rate she hadn't adhered to her exercise schedule in a couple of weeks, and she needed to air the cobwebs out of her head. Running or walking several miles each week gave her time to think.

Thinking. She did far too much of that these days. *Really, I ought to get out more.* As the thought crossed her mind, so did the double meaning. Not only did she need to exercise more often, she needed to socialize too. The few evenings out with Evan broke the ice of her self-imposed hiatus from dating.

It was a good thing Evan had no idea how frequently she thought about him. He didn't seem like the kind of guy in dire need of ego pumping. Evan exuded confidence in a big way, and he wasn't the kind of man who took no for an answer.

He had been nothing but a gentleman after the pizza debacle. Perhaps they should try for the championship wrestling circuit. They had their moves down pretty well. She and Evan could be a formidable tag team.

Still, a line remained between them. Business on one side, pleasure on the other. Evan had nudged and she had bent her rules a bit. But they hadn't quite bridged the gap between them. Evan seemed to be waiting for her to take the initiative. Since she had placed the line there, it was up to her to remove it altogether.

Before he'd left last night he turned to her. He took off her glasses and handed them to her before cupping her face in his hands. And then he kissed her. A nice, slow kiss which made her toes tingle and a rush of heat spread through her body. Before she'd completely recovered he was gone, and she stood there clutching her glasses, hardly realizing she'd bent the frames.

The man was absolutely aggravating! He knew what he was doing, he was showing her what she could have if she'd cross that line. Instead of getting behind her and shoving her across, he left the decision in her hands. Evan Delaford was devious in the most caring sort of way. Kind of like her mother.

Forty-five minutes later, with a tiny amount of endorphins kicking in, she made her way back home. The cool shower felt good, and once again she felt in control. She would not allow this . . . diversion . . . to undermine her comfort level. But what a diversion. She pictured Evan in all his various guises. As the high-powered executive in the buttoned-down business suit at their first meeting, and casual, with stubble on his jaw and those torn jeans.

What on earth was wrong with the man? How could he possibly think he looked bad? And last night, clean-cut but casual. A perfect combination of both. No doubt about it. She liked what she saw any way she looked at it.

The phone rang and Evan's image faded from her thoughts. Who would call her at home in the middle of a weekday afternoon?

"Hello?"

"Hello, dear. I'm surprised you're home so early."

"Hi, Mom. What a surprise to hear from you, too. I took the afternoon off. I needed some space and time to myself. Things have been a bit hectic lately."

Perhaps Vivian might take the hint, but as soon as Liz heard the intake of breath, the words "no such luck" circulated in her brain.

"I was curious how things went with that young man yesterday. I got home late from bridge last night or I would have called. And I know how you hate to be bothered with personal calls at work."

Liz made a face at the thought of yesterday's fiasco with Kenny. Rarely did she engage in such juvenile behavior. Speaking of juvenile . . .

"Mom, did you meet this Kenny before you arranged for me to have lunch with him?"

"Well, no, dear. There really wasn't time. But I

spoke to him at length over the phone. He seemed like a very nice young man."

Infantile was the word to describe Kenny-with-no-last-name. "He's young, Mom. He may be twenty-two or twenty-three, but it was hard to tell from the way he behaved."

"That's only a ten-year age difference, dear. There's nothing wrong with a summer/fall romance, is there?"

"No, but there's something wrong with Kenny. Thanks anyway, Mom."

"Not even for the one night? The awards banquet?"

Liz tried to imagine Kenny in such an atmosphere. She'd probably have to tote a diaper bag filled with towelettes and toys to wipe up the spills and keep him entertained.

"Mom, trust me. I met him. He'd feel out of place at such a formal function." *Besides,* Liz thought, *all those women and jangling jewelry at once would probably be too much for him.* She didn't want to be responsible for Kenny's sensory overload.

"Oh, dear! I so hoped this one would work out."

"Really, Mom, you're giving this event much more importance than it deserves."

"Liz," her mother said in the patient tone Liz was so familiar with, chuckling a bit and making Liz remember exactly what it felt like to be seven years old, "this is your big night. You need to find a date, dear."

"I don't think so. Thanks for your concern, though. I'll keep working on it."

"I still think my suggestion the other day is a good one."

Oh no, Liz cringed. *Which suggestion? The one about her clothes? Her hair?*

"Which suggestion was that, Mom?" She asked, dreading the answer, yet anxious to hear. At times, Vivian's thinking fascinated Liz. In another life, her mother would have made a great criminal mastermind. Vivian was so . . . devious, in that thoroughly thoughtful way of hers.

"I'm referring to the young man you met in Goodtimes last week. You remember," Vivian nudged gently in her most maternal fashion.

When Liz did not acknowledge at once, Vivian continued.

"You do remember, dear," Vivian said in an insistently conspiratorial tone. "Very good-looking. Dark hair. Nice eyes. He was leaving the table as I returned from the restroom. His name is Evan, didn't you say?"

Not willing to let her mother know she had been thinking about him too, she acknowledged the name.

"Oh yes. Evan. I remember him," she said, and let it go at that.

"I think he'd look absolutely superb in a tuxedo, dear. You know," she confided, "formal wear makes any man more attractive, but that particular young man, well, he'd look outstanding."

And how, Liz thought, as her teeth clenched. She would not respond. *Evening wear? Good grief, the man looks superb in anything. Business suits, jeans, T-shirts. Most likely, he would look superb no matter what he wore.*

"Yes, Mother," she agreed. "I know exactly what

you mean. That's just it. Evan looks too good. Period.
You know how I feel about handsome men. I don't
want to be used and tossed away when a more attractive woman catches his eye."

"Now Liz, you shouldn't judge the poor man based
on looks alone. You're a librarian, after all. Don't you
know you can't judge a book by its cover?"

Liz winced. She absolutely hated her mother's
common-sense lectures—almost as much as she hated
when her mother was right. "What about you, Mom?"
she interrupted, before Vivian had a chance to get going on this particular speech.

"I already have a date. Thank you for asking, dear,"
replied Vivian, quite civilly despite Liz's rude question.

"You can always invite Kenny. Since he's not my
type, you're welcome to him." Liz said wickedly, unable to resist. The mental picture was just too perfect.

"Oh no, dear. I'm sure Kenny is a nice enough
young man, but judging by what you've told me he's
not my type either."

Liz reflected on that one for a moment, and wondered again why her mother thought Kenny would be
her type. It was difficult thinking of Kenny as being
anyone's type.

"Well, who are you going with?" pressed Liz, as
her mother neglected to fill in that bit of information.
Why should Vivian be let off the hook without a taste
of her own medicine?

"I'm going with Judge Kramer. You remember
him—he and your father used to play golf together."

"Yes, I remember him. He's very nice. Cute, too. Congratulations, Mom. So, Judge Kramer doesn't have a friend for me?"

"No, he didn't . . . how did you know I'd asked him?" Vivian demanded, as her daughter burst out laughing.

"The word is out, Mom. No unattached male in this city is safe from Vivian Brady's search. Don't worry, Mom. It will work out. I'll have a date. I won't embarrass you. And, by the way, you'd better plan on wearing low-heeled shoes. If I remember correctly, Judge Kramer was into serious ballroom dancing competitions at one time."

That ought to keep her busy, Liz thought as she hung up. She smiled at the thought of Vivian practicing her tango, only to be replaced with the picture of Evan Delaford looking divine in his tuxedo. She simply could not will away that image, no matter how hard she tried.

It didn't do much for Liz's battered ego to learn her fifty-something mother had found a date in no time, while she herself was no closer than she had been three weeks ago. Mentally she ran through the possibilities. Her cousin Lenny? No. Joey Patrillo? Unfortunately, she had noticed his wedding ring. Randy Hollander? Engaged to the redhead, and she was welcome to him. Kenny? Liz shuddered at the thought.

She and Evan Delaford were friends, weren't they? What could it hurt? She needed an unattached, presentable and willing escort. Evan fit the bill perfectly. She would ask him, she decided, because she had no options left.

Chapter Eleven

An hour went by while Liz paced back and forth, rehearsing lines in her head. *Why,* she wondered, *does the thought of approaching Evan Delaford for a favor fill me with terror?* She had done the same for him, hadn't she? Well, not quite, she admitted. It was one thing to meet in a restaurant under the guise of business, and quite another to be her escort to a formal awards banquet.

Why was she so nervous? It wasn't as if she was asking him for a date. Not really. What if he said no? She had nothing to lose except her pride. If he said no, she'd be embarrassed and disappointed but no worse off than she was now. Her mother could be counted on to dig up a date for her at the last minute. That final thought mobilized her courage.

Twice she reached for the phone and pulled back,

as if from a heated iron. A glance at the clock reminded her it was still business hours. Evan would be working. With any luck, he wouldn't be in his room. She could leave a message. If he was interested enough to call back, by that time she'd have her nerves under control. She wouldn't feel like a teenager asking him out.

It's not a date, she reminded herself once again. But since she had turned him down, there was no reason for him to be generous with her. She did her best to keep him off-balance, because that's the way he made her feel.

The third time she reached for the phone, she managed to dial the hotel number. The peculiar blip-blip sounds of the hotel phone rang in her ear, and after six blips she relaxed, mentally preparing the message she would leave for him. She waited for the hotel operator to pick up again.

"Delaford."

After six rings he answered. Liz was stunned. He shouldn't be there. She wasn't prepared for this!

"Hello? Is someone there?"

Oh no, she thought. *Speak! Don't let him get away.* This was it. Evan was on the line. Now what? How ridiculous she felt.

"Evan? Hi." Her voice came out shaky and unnaturally high-pitched.

"Liz! What a surprise. Is everything all right?"

"No. I mean, yes. Why would you think something was wrong?"

"You're calling me. Distinctly out of character. So what's up?"

He had a wonderful voice, Liz thought. She stopped listening to his words and let the sound of his voice wash over her. Warm and smooth, like mulled cider. He sounded like he was smiling. Could it be he didn't mind her call?

"Liz?"

"Mmm?"

"Are you still with me?"

Snapping out of her reverie, she was annoyed that she'd allowed herself to be transported by the mere sound of his voice. It was positively hypnotic. Perhaps this wasn't such a great idea. But she was committed to going through with it. She paced back and forth next to the bed, unable to sit while she approached the moment of truth.

"Sorry, I was distracted. I'm kind of surprised to find you there."

"You mean you called, thinking I wouldn't be here. And then you'd be off the hook?"

How did he do that? He shouldn't be able to read her mind.

"No, I was sort of hoping you would be but . . . I thought you'd probably be working."

"I am."

"And I'm interrupting you."

"Answering the phone to find you on the other end is the best thing that's happened to me all day. Please don't apologize."

"Okay, I'm sorry."

Evan chuckled and Liz relaxed a notch, sure that he wasn't laughing *at* her. "I have a business proposition for you," she began.

"A business proposition?"

"Yes. That is, if you'll still be in town through next weekend. A week from Saturday night, actually."

"A week from this Saturday?" he repeated after her.

She closed her eyes, praying for patience. Hearing Evan breathing on the line was a trial. The image of him grinning at her discomfort, well. . . .

"Yes. A week from this coming Saturday."

"Let me check." There was silence followed by the sound of pages turning. She never considered he might be gone by then. Or busy. Her face felt hot to the touch. Why hadn't she considered he might have a previous engagement? Unbeknownst to Cindy, she had read the entire *Business Journal* article, along with everything else ever written about Evan Delaford. He was single, successful, wealthy, and popular with the ladies. Beautiful, accomplished, sophisticated women. Evan could have his pick. There had been nothing in anything Liz read which mentioned a possible penchant Evan might have for poorly dressed small-town librarians who constantly rewrote their own dating rule manuals. A wave of doubt washed over her.

"I can be here a week from this Saturday."

His response barely registered. Get out! Get out now, while you still can, Liz's scrambled brain screamed. "You know what, Evan? Never mind, okay? I don't know what I was thinking."

"You were thinking you had a business proposition

that I'd be interested in," Evan reminded her, not bothering to disguise his interest. "What is it?" Evan wouldn't let go.

"Well," she said, removing a fingernail from her mouth, where it had replaced a knuckle, "you know how I went with you to check out the restaurants?"

"I'm not likely to forget anytime soon," Evan assured her, a smile in his voice. "You have a way of turning a simple dinner date into a memorable event."

"It's a gift," Liz quipped, smiling at their easy banter, her earlier insecurity forgotten. If she wasn't careful, he was going to distract her again. Taking a deep breath, she dove in. "I have to attend this awards banquet, and I was hoping, as sort of a *quid pro quo,* uh, you know, since I did you a favor now you could do the same for me . . ."

"I'm not your friend Kenny. I know the meaning of *quid pro quo.* Modern Latin. Something for something. One thing in return for another."

As if she hadn't heard a word he said, she continued rambling on. "I hoped you could do me a favor and go with me." There. It was out. She could breathe again.

"I would be honored," he said.

"If you don't have anything else scheduled, that is. Your social calendar is probably full, though, and I certainly wouldn't expect you to rearrange anything. I just thought on the off chance you were free and if it wouldn't be too inconvenient for you."

Her back was now against the wall near the bathroom. She was hyperventilating. Nerves giving out all at once, she slid down the wall and collapsed into a position not unlike that of a beached jellyfish.

"Wait. Did you just say yes?" When had her brain switched to seven-second-delay mode? Her cheeks burned. She was becoming an expert in looking like a fool in front of Evan Delaford. She sat up straighter.

"No," he replied. "I said I would be honored. I'd like very much to go to the awards banquet with you a week from this Saturday."

"Oh. You would?" Was that it? "Thanks." She paused, not knowing how to respond after the fact. "I forgot to mention," she continued, "it's black tie."

"No problem. So what's the formal affair?"

"Affair? Who said anything about an affair?"

"I did. Wishful thinking, evidently. Forgive me." Evan sounded not at all repentant.

Liz tried to steer the conversation back to safe territory. "It's a state-wide civic awards banquet. Dinner. Speeches. Dancing."

"It's not a masquerade ball, is it?"

"No, of course not. What ever gave you that idea?"

"I just wanted to be clear on the dress code," he continued in the same reasonable tone of voice. "No need for a disguise, right?"

"Right."

"And that includes you?"

"Of course," Liz answered, her brow furrowing.

"Well, then. I'm definitely looking forward to it."

"What does that mean?"

"Only that I've been wanting to see the real Liz Brady since the day I met you."

"What do you mean 'the real Liz Brady'?"

He paused for just a moment. She swore she could hear him smiling. "It means I'm counting on finally seeing you without your gray sweater. Don't let me down, Liz."

Evan just tossed down the sartorial gauntlet. He was smiling during their phone conversation—Liz was sure of it. But he'd have no reason to find her appearance amusing next Saturday night. Evan would be surprised, and that would make everything she endured since meeting him worthwhile. The teasing, amused look would be wiped off of Evan Delaford's handsome face. She didn't want a confused frown from him, either. She wanted to see appreciation in his gaze. Perhaps they could get through an entire evening without knocking their heads together.

Up until now, she had been a challenge to him, because she didn't fall all over him as every other woman in his life probably did. To Evan she was a novelty, a diversion. A woman who went out of her way not to impress him. Well, next Saturday she'd either impress him or die trying.

From her bureau she pulled out lacy underthings and put them on. Reaching into the depths of her closet, she removed a garment bag. She laid it carefully on the bed and unzipped it. There it was, just as she remembered. The black Vera Wang she'd never had occasion to wear.

It was a shimmering bit of silk worked magically into a slim sheath of a long gown, with tiny straps and a high slit up the left leg. She fell in love with it at first sight on a trip to New York City. The county sent her to attend a conference on computer filing systems, but she couldn't resist the temptation to browse in all of those wonderful stores. She found the original Saks Fifth Avenue, then she discovered Madison Avenue. She was in heaven.

In spite of her then newly adopted dress code, she tried on this dress. She didn't have a clue when she would ever have the opportunity to wear it, and the price tag should have given her pause, but it didn't. The black Vera Wang had been made for her.

She transformed into someone else the moment she zipped it up. No one would recognize Ms. Brady from the library when she walked into the ballroom wearing this dress. Good. The "real" Liz Brady was back, big time.

As she studied herself in the mirror, she decided this black tie event was going to be a lot of fun.

Chapter Twelve

"When do you land?" Paul asked. "You seem rather reluctant to leave Rockleigh. Is there something going on down there I should know about? Problems?"

"You know everything I do," replied Evan. "You're the one who wanted me back in the office to compare notes, remember?" He stretched his long legs out in front of him and relaxed back into the seat. He had labored long and hard these past ten years to build his company into what it was today. Having a corporate jet at his beck and call was one recent reward he felt he deserved after all the blood and sweat he'd put into his career since college.

"Yes, but as I recall, you never do anything I suggest without interrogating me first," his partner reminded him. "Either you've changed your habits, which I would find strange, since you've been a dedicated creature of habit ever since I've known you. Or something is going on. By the way, how's your librarian friend?"

Good grief, thought Evan. He didn't want Paul to quiz him about Liz.

"Uh, sorry Paul. I have to go now. I can barely hear you. The signal's breaking up." He crackled the wrapper from a package of peanuts close to the mouthpiece of the phone. "I should be there in a couple of hours."

Whew! That was a close one. Until he figured out what was going on with his "librarian friend" he was certainly in no position to discuss her with anyone else.

Evan went directly to the office from the airport. Since he planned to return to Rockleigh in a couple of days, he'd kept his room and left his luggage at the hotel. He had a number of things he had to take care of back at the apartment, including making sure his evening wear was ready. Maybe he should get a haircut? No, he thought, his idea to dress down had appealed to Liz. Still, this was a formal event. Perhaps a trim.

Evan climbed out of the cab and hurried into the building. He waved at the security desk, and out of the corner of his eye saw the guard pick up the phone. Full alert. Boss on the way!

The elevator climbed directly to the fortieth floor, and he smiled at the receptionist as he passed.

"Good morning, Mr. Delaford."

"Good morning, Peggy. I'll be in with Mr. Stratford. Please hold his calls."

"All right, sir."

A familiar surge of energy raced through him as he strode down the hall toward Paul's office. Evan loved his work. He enjoyed setting wheels in motion, putting deals together, being on top of things, making money. Sometimes the biggest deals were done with a simple handshake. That's what it was all about in business, he thought. In the end it came down to a man's reputation. A man's word.

He greeted Paul's secretary and whipped open the door to his partner's office. "Hey Paul, I told you I'd be here in time for lunch."

Paul glanced up from behind his desk, looking as if he'd rather be any place but where he was just now. He ruffled his hand through his hair and pulled at his beard, giving Evan an apologetic look as he stood.

"There you are, Evan darling! I am so glad you're home." Catching him off-guard, Aileen Summers rose from the chair next to Paul's desk and vaulted into Evan's arms. Had she performed gymnastics during the talent portion of those numerous beauty pageants? Evan wondered. Or was she just warming up for the next Olympics?

"How long has it been, Evan? Two weeks? Three? You've been working so hard! Such a hush-hush deal, Paul wouldn't even give me your phone number!"

God bless Paul, Evan thought, giving the man himself a grateful look while his arms were still full of Aileen and the cloying, heavy floral scent she preferred. "And you didn't call me once," she pouted prettily as he disengaged himself.

"It's nice to see you, Aileen. You look well. What brings you here?"

" 'Nice'! 'Well'! Did you hear that?" She turned to Paul, eyeing him malevolently, as if it was his fault Evan hadn't given her the compliment she considered her due. "Darling," she said, turning back to Evan, "I hardly look like a recovering patient by any means. I tried to make myself perfect for you today. I hope I look a little better than 'well'."

"Right. You do, Aileen, but I'm pressed for time. I didn't expect to see you. Paul and I have two weeks' worth to review. I wish I had more time, but we're snowed under, right, Paul?"

Paul had no problem booting Aileen out of the office while Evan used his smile and every bit of charm he possessed to defuse her formidable temper.

"Sorry, Aileen," Paul agreed, not sounding sorry at all. "Evan's right. Things have piled up while he's been out of town."

"You can at least have lunch with me, can't you?" she asked Evan.

"I'm sorry." Evan found it difficult to work even the smallest note of regret into his voice. The last person he wanted to spend time with was Aileen Summers, and the absolute last thing he wanted to do today was have lunch with her.

Aileen silently took measure of what she was up against, and changed her approach. "I understand how it is, Evan. After all, I'm on deadline too. I simply must have a private word with you. I won't keep you but a minute, I promise. Can we go into another room where we can talk?"

What now? wondered Evan. Something was up, but it was better sometimes to go along. "Of course. Let's step into my office. I didn't realize this was an emergency."

Aileen looked the tiniest bit embarrassed. "Oh, no, Evan, it's not an emergency. Unless you count the fact that I'm dying to spend some quality time with you. But I *do* need you to check your schedule for a specific date." She squeezed one of his biceps meaningfully as they entered his office.

Evan's corner office offered a magnificent view of the lake spread out in the distance. The city of Chicago was vibrantly alive below. Aileen looked lovely as usual, in a chic tailored suit, and her long, honey blond hair fluffed and puffed just so. She wore makeup, a lot of it, expertly applied. Evan never quite realized what an involved process it was until one occasion when Aileen took nearly an hour to "add a touch of color" to her cheeks.

Evan poured a glass of cold water from a full pitcher on the side table as a ploy to put some distance between them. "Forgive me," he said, "I'm very thirsty from the flight. May I get you something?"

"No, thank you, Evan. I don't want to keep you. Can you check your schedule for a week from Saturday? I have a charity ball to attend—some awards function in some little town in the middle of nowhere, and I need an escort. I hoped we could go together.

I'm representing the station, so I'll be busy," she warned, "but it would be nice for us to spend some time together. We hardly get to see each other any more. I've missed you."

"Why don't we sit over here?" he suggested, and led the way to the sitting area. The couch was long, deep and comfortable, and had been one of Evan's priorities, since he spent numerous late nights alternately working and sleeping there.

He took a long sip of the ice water, and as he looked at Aileen, he wondered what about her had ever interested him. In Aileen's eyes, he was nothing more than a fashion accessory. Maybe at one time, that's what she had been for him as well. But it wasn't enough. Not anymore.

"We don't see each other because we're both busy, Aileen. You're running around on assignments. I have a feeling that pretty soon we'll be seeing you on one of the networks."

Aileen visibly perked up. "Network" to a local television reporter was the ultimate success story, and Evan knew this was what Aileen had her eye on. She set her sights on the evening news slot four years ago, and that's where she planned to be shortly. That, and, of course, marrying Evan Delaford. She preened as she answered him.

"I have been talking to several people, so it is definitely a possibility. But I don't want to discuss work now. We can chat about business later, over dinner, perhaps? Meanwhile, what about that date?"

Rather than prolong the discomfort, Evan came right out with it.

"I'm sorry, Aileen. I have a previous commitment that evening."

"But I checked with your secretary, and there's nothing on your calendar . . ." She bit her lip as she revealed how much research she had done to find out his schedule.

"Beverly didn't know about it."

"Are you sure? It's the twenty-third. Maybe you should double check the date," Aileen suggested.

"I don't need to check the date, Aileen. I'm positively booked that night."

"But how could you be? You've been out in the sticks somewhere for weeks, haven't you? Speaking of sticks, this thing I have to go to is in some little town I never even heard of, and believe me, I'm not looking forward to it. What a drag to be stuck in the middle of nowhere! The station refuses to let me use the helicopter, and there are no flights back until morning. So, I'll be stuck there overnight." She pouted as she contemplated this course of events. "I so looked forward to you being there with me. But, I guess it will have to be next time."

"Aileen?"

"Yes?" she said, as she stood and smoothed out the wrinkles from her skirt.

"We had a conversation several weeks before I left," he said, not unkindly. "We decided we'd see other people, right? We agreed we have no future as a couple."

"I remember the conversation, Evan, but I don't recall agreeing to anything. Besides, you've said things like that before. I understand you get distracted sometimes because of work. I don't mind."

He stood and shook his head. "I'm sorry, Aileen. I meant what I said."

"Are you seeing someone else?"

He thought about that. Well, it was the truth. He was seeing Liz. Or at least he was trying to, and she seemed agreeable as long as it was on her terms. He had decided he could live with those terms for a while longer. At least until she came to her senses and realized their relationship went much deeper and extended far beyond mere friendship. Technically he supposed he wasn't seeing anyone in the way Aileen meant, but he hoped to remedy that in the near future. "Yes," he answered her simply.

If his answer disappointed Aileen she hid it well. "That's too bad, Evan. We were great together. I want you to know I won't hold this against you when you change your mind."

He couldn't say he felt sorry for hurting her feelings, because to date he saw little evidence of any to hurt. Aileen reminded him of a shark, constantly swimming and feeding, always ready to move on to the next advantageous . . . liaison. There was no need to rationalize with a shark, and there was no need to do so with Aileen. Until he took himself off the market permanently, she'd probably continue swimming by every now and again just to test the waters.

"I won't change my mind. Take it from me, though,

the middle of nowhere's not really so bad. You might meet someone new."

She looked at him as if he had lost his mind. "Now I *know* you've spent too much time away from Chicago. I hope things work out for you Evan. But don't lose my number."

Then she was out the door, and onto another fish in the sea.

Although Evan kept busy, the days seemed to drag. Chicago lacked its usual appeal. He was restless and easily distracted, and generally out of sorts. Perhaps if he kept his mind on the work at hand instead of on Liz Brady his mood would improve. Had small-town life gotten to him these past couple of weeks? Or was it who was in that small town which made him anxious to get back?

Resolutely, he stuck to his normal routine. Up early for a run along the lake with Casey. The big retriever was delirious that the master of the house had returned. Evan was lucky Paul had a wife and kids who loved the dog almost as much as he did, and didn't mind keeping Casey when Evan traveled. After his run, each day was spent in the office, reviewing what had gone on while he was away.

Paul had done an excellent job. Evan pretty much knew where everything stood but once he was back in the office, his phone rang constantly. Clients wanted to talk to Evan. His presence, as well as his opinions, reassured them.

"Yes, Walter, that's correct. Absolutely. I look forward to seeing you in a couple of weeks. We'll go out for that steak dinner at Milo's. They've got a filet that melts in your mouth. You take care, now."

What a way to spend a Saturday afternoon. The office was quiet, and he looked at the phone, which was finally still. What was Liz doing right now? he wondered. Over the past couple of days he thought a lot about her. He decided Chicago wasn't any different— *he* was the one who had changed. After thirty-odd years in his hometown, he felt a bit lost and alone. Somehow, he was going to convince Liz to come and visit him. He would show her around, let her see what life was like in the city. She'd enjoy it, he knew. Maybe she'd let him take her shopping for some new clothes. He smiled at the thought of her in her huge sweater and those oversized dresses.

Then reality set in. When was he going to tell her he met her through her mother? It was only a matter of time until she learned the facts. He didn't want to keep it from her; not really. Not unless she was going to be a stickler and refuse to go out with him because of still another rule.

Evan had never met such a contrary woman. Liz must have had a very bad experience to make her set up these ridiculous rules for herself. He could imagine her seated at her desk and writing them down. *Rule Number One: I will not dress to attract men. Rule Number Two: If a man appears interested in me, it better not be because of the way I look. Rule Number Three: I will not date men whom I find attractive.* He hated Rule Number Three, because Liz's attraction to him was so transparent she had nearly succumbed before she remembered it was against the rules! *Rule Number Four: I will not date any man my mother arranges for me to meet.* Evan wasn't too crazy about this one, either. He could just imagine Liz's addendums to Rule Number Four: *Rule Number Four will still apply even if my mother arranges for me to meet Evan Delaford; even if I am wildly attracted to him; even if he's crazy about me.* And it would go on from there. Liz simply had too many rules, and she seemed to make them up as she went along. The good thing about rules, though, Evan reminded himself, was that they were made to be broken.

What was in her rulebook about Evan Delaford calling her? When should he call her? Now? Tonight? Tomorrow? And since when had he ever played by anyone else's rules? It was time to stop this nonsense. Grabbing the bag he always kept ready in the closet with his gear, he headed out to his athletic club to work off some frustration.

"Evan?"

"Paul? What time is it?"

"Eight-thirty."

"In the morning? It's Sunday, isn't it?"

"Sorry. I just had a call from Roger Gorman at Goodtimes. You know, the restaurant chain where you've been eating yourself silly?"

"Right." He sat up, instantly awake. Even if it was a Sunday morning, this was business.

"The owners reached an agreement late last night.

On all terms. They're looking to finalize the deal by the first of the year. What did you say to them?"

"Nothing special. We just talked. They were surprised to hear how much I knew about their operation—down to the number of croutons they put on a Caesar salad."

Paul chuckled. "So you impressed them with your thorough research."

"Right. That must have been it. It's a decent operation. It should do well in the average American city. Considering the competition, I think it's got a better-than-average shot at success. You could do a lot worse for a place to go on a Saturday night date."

"They're overnighting the contracts, so I'll need to call Jorgenson in the morning so he can get the legal ball rolling. Oh, by the way, I bumped into Aileen last night at Romy's."

Evan knew Paul and his wife favored Romy's, the city's latest hot spot and eatery. "And?"

"Nothing. I guess she didn't take you permanently dumping her too hard—she was babysitting the Blackhawks' newest rookie. It seemed to work for her."

"You know Aileen. Any port in a storm. She gets tossed from one, she bounces right into the next."

"Yeah. Well. I didn't think she'd give up on you so easily, though." Paul sounded a little dubious. "You'll be in town the rest of the week, right?."

"Now that the deal's done, I have no reason to leave."

"Good. I'll see you tomorrow, then. First thing."

* * *

After contemplating his options for dinner, Evan stuck a frozen pizza in the oven. Though dining alone was hardly a new experience for him, he had no desire to go out. He didn't feel much like ordering something in, either. All he wanted to do was get through the weekend, through the week, and back to Rockleigh, Illinois.

Who was he kidding? He wanted to solve the mystery of what made Liz Brady tick. At the rate he was going, it might take a lifetime to figure her out, a possibility which had definite appeal.

After flicking through fifty channels of cable television, he looked at the phone. It was nine-thirty. She should be in. He dialed her number.

"Hello?" said a sleepy-sounding Liz.

"Did I wake you?"

"Evan?"

Now this was a treat for the ego. *Who else was she expecting to call?* he wondered.

"Yep. How are you?"

"I'm fine. Is everything all right?"

"Absolutely. Listen, the Goodtimes deal is happening. I got the word this weekend."

"Oh, that's great. Does that mean that you don't have to come back to Rockleigh?"

Was it worry he heard in her voice? Or relief? "No, no. I'll fly in at the end of the week. I wanted to make sure we were still on for Saturday night." Liar. What he wanted was to hear the sound of her voice.

"I plan on it. Unless you've had a better offer."

"I don't think I'll ever get a better offer." *Where*

did that come from? Evan wondered. And what exactly did he mean by it? He hadn't spoken so often without thinking first since—well, never. Liz was obviously baffled by his comment too, for she said nothing.

"We're going to sign the deal next week. I wanted to have a final go at the salad bar. You know, I'm not convinced they need one since they have such an extensive salad menu. But I could be wrong. Interested in keeping me company?"

"And miss out on the deciding moment? Not a chance."

"Good. I'll try to get in early on Friday afternoon, and I'll call you then."

He hung up the phone, turned off the light, and felt much better after hearing her voice.

He made a mental note to check out all the salad dressings on Friday. He would be having dinner with Liz, so he'd better pack an extra set of clothes, too, just in case things got out of hand. That was the last thought to cross his mind as he drifted off to sleep.

Chapter Thirteen

Liz gave in to Vivian, and joined her at Susie's Kut & Kurl on Saturday morning. Her feet were propped on a stool, with cotton wound between her toes, while the manicurist completed her pedicure. Barely able to resist pulling away, she giggled as the feather-like touches sent her tickle reflex into high-gear.

"This is torture, Mom. I don't know how you do this every week," she grumbled good-naturedly to Vivian, who sat next to her.

"It doesn't look right to go out in sandals without a proper pedicure. I thought I taught you as much growing up, but it seems like you girls do what you want. What about tips? Long nails look so elegant with evening wear..."

"I don't care for talons, Mother. Nails get in the

123

way. Make it difficult to file away all those books, in case you haven't noticed."

"Well, at least have a manicure so your hands will look nice. I don't understand," she said, staring pointedly at her daughter's head, "why you're not having your hair done as well. Why ever not?"

"I had it trimmed," Liz pointed out defensively. "But I can style it just as well as a hairdresser, and they always use too much hairspray."

Vivian mumbled something under her breath, so Liz took the cautious route and intently studied her left hand, thinking back to last night's conversation with Evan. He refused to cooperate when she told him she could meet him at the hotel where the awards dinner was held. She wanted to spare him the trouble of calling for her. After all, she reflected, this was a business arrangement. He was simply repaying her for her help, but he wouldn't hear of it.

"Are you trying to ruin my reputation?" demanded Evan, after their second trip to Goodtimes' salad bar the previous evening.

"How would I do that?"

"Don't you think I have any manners whatsoever? I was taught to call at my date's home for her."

"But this isn't a date," she protested.

He was adamant. "Nevertheless, I'll pick you up. You know it's not a date, and I know it's not a date, but Liz, have a care for my public image. You asked me to escort you, right? Besides, I did it your way, remember? We met at the restaurants. Now it's my turn. Okay?"

Liz wondered what Evan Delaford's mother was like. Could she be anything like Vivian? Would she ever have dared to set up her gorgeous, unattached son? She blew that thought off as quickly as it had come—a man who looked like Evan would never have a problem attracting women.

So it was arranged. He would collect her at her house at five o'clock. Five would come so quickly, she thought, as the manicurist put the final touch on her toenails. She felt the adrenaline starting to flow. Getting ready for a formal event was truly exciting.

Along with the excitement came anticipation. She wanted to see how Mr. Evan Delaford looked in a tux.

"Liz!"

Suddenly her attention was drawn back to the present, and she was aware of the sharp, unpleasant smell of the polish the manicurist was applying to her mother's nails.

"So, you won't tell me what you're wearing?" cajoled Vivian for the fourth time since they'd arrived nearly an hour earlier.

"No. It's a surprise."

"As long as it doesn't include that mousy gray sweater as an accessory, I'll be thrilled to death. Is it new?" she asked, continuing in her inimitable way to glean bits of information.

"Not exactly. Something I picked up in New York last year while I was at that conference. I've never had an opportunity to wear it before now."

"Ahh," said Vivian, nodding her head perceptively, "before you and Randy . . ."

"Yes, Mother. Before we broke up."

"So it will be something tasteful and attractive. Like the clothes you *used* to wear."

Liz was determined nothing would put a damper on her big day, not even her mother's barb, so she let that one slide with a sigh, and admired the shade of creamy red on her nails.

"I'm so pleased your friend Evan is able to come with you tonight."

"Mmmm," Liz replied in acknowledgment, and nothing more. From her tone, Liz recognized her mother's attempt to change the topic with a subtle invitation for Liz to confess all, but Liz resisted and remained lost in her thoughts.

Going down her mental checklist, she had everything she needed for tonight. Funny how things work out. She should be nervous about speaking in front of a room full of five hundred strangers. But no—all her thoughts were on getting herself ready. She couldn't wait to see Evan's reaction. She wanted to see a look of surprise on his handsome face. Liz wanted him to see the "real" Liz Brady. Interesting, how she now thought of her previous image as the real Liz. In some strange way over the past week or so she grew comfortable with the thought of looking "good" again by other people's standards. *I guess Evan is responsible for that,* she thought, since he pursued her even without all the trimmings.

Her nails dry, she stood up. "Gotta run," she said, kissing Vivian on the cheek. "I'll see you and your dapper date tonight." She could have sworn Vivian blushed, just the tiniest bit.

"I look forward to it," replied Vivian, a contented smile on her lips as she inspected both hands.

Liz spent the afternoon with a book, too wound up to eat or nap. Each time she glanced at the clock, it seemed only five minutes later than the last peek. Finally, at three-thirty, she decided to get ready.

After a leisurely shower she studied her face in the bathroom mirror.

First things first. Her contacts. It was a while since she wore them, and it took several tries before she got the first one in properly. The other lens went in perfectly on the first try. She remembered why she had gone to contacts in the first place. Her eyes seemed to be magnified by them, their color more startlingly green.

The bathroom drawer where she stowed her make-up was stuck. Not surprising. She hadn't opened it all summer. "Arghh!" Liz groaned as she tugged on the drawer handle. "Come on, you. Not now." She braced herself with one hand on the sink, and the other firmly wrapped around the handle of the stubborn drawer and yanked as hard as she could. The drawer popped free with a sudden snap and landed upended on the bathroom floor with a clatter. "Oh no!" Liz jammed her thumb in her mouth, sucking on the ragged nail. Her perfect manicure ruined! Now she would have to file it and search for polish in a shade close enough to match. She bent to right the drawer and pick up the strewn tubes of lipstick, cases of blusher and powder, bottles of foundation, and eye and lip pencils.

Twenty minutes later she smiled at the face reflected in the mirror. She subscribed to the theory that less is more when it came to makeup. She much preferred sophisticated subtlety to overdone and obvious.

She slipped into her underwear, then sat down to put on her silk stockings. *It's a funny thing,* she thought, as she slid the stocking up her right leg, *how such a tiny bit of silk can transform one's self-image.* Whenever she wore stockings she felt downright glamorous.

The dress was perfect. She would wear a black silk shawl draped over her shoulders. It was a good thing Evan insisted on picking her up, so she wouldn't freeze walking across the parking lot!

She was ready ahead of schedule. At four-thirty she started pacing. She checked her appearance in the mirror several times. The mirror reflected her image, but inside she felt like an elegant fairy princess. Perhaps she'd have a fairy tale evening with a handsome prince. Or maybe her finery would turn to rags and her ride into a pumpkin at the stroke of midnight.

She did her hair in a classic upsweep, but she let it air dry to encourage the curls at the ends. Those curls always caught Evan's attention. The corkscrew tendrils lay loosely at the nape of her neck, and one peeked out over her shoulder as if inviting further attention.

Falling from a thin gold chain around her neck was the gift from her father on her twenty-first birthday, a one-carat diamond solitaire. At the time he'd given it to her, he joked that if she ever needed cash in a hurry, she could always trade it in. They all laughed, and the bittersweet memory was made much more poignant by the fact that he passed away soon afterward.

He'd planned to give all three girls such necklaces, special coming-of-age gifts. Liz wore no other jewelry except for an opal, her birthstone, on her right hand.

At the sound of the doorbell, she started. Her heart hammered. She forced herself to take slow, deep breaths.

Over the weekend she had practiced various femme fatale poses in front of the mirror. When she greeted Evan at the door in this dress, she was determined to knock his socks off. She wanted to be cool and sophisticated, so Evan Delaford would fall at her feet. Her moment of truth had arrived.

She opened the door and struck her pose, one hand extended in the air regally, the opposite hand on her hip which she had thrust forward, arching her back, her chin held high. "This is the *real* Liz Brady, in the flesh," she announced proudly.

"Huh? Oh, yeah, Brady, right."

Liz's chin dropped a notch as she gazed at the individual on the threshold. A rather grimy T-shirt barely covered his belly, and baggy blue jeans hung low on his hips. The sloppy end of a well-chewed cigar hung from between slack lips. He was short and balding. Faded blue eyes twinkled at her. "Sorry for the disturbance, ma'am." He nodded in Liz's direction. "I'm with the phone company." He indicated his I.D.,

Curly, pinned to his chest. "Been reports of problems with the phone lines in the area. I need to check your wiring."

"You—what?"

"Won't take but a minute, ma'am," Curly explained apologetically, looking Liz up and down while chewing on the damp cigar butt. "Need to check your lines."

"But—but, I'm not having any trouble with my phone," Liz insisted.

"Yes, ma'am," Curly acknowledged as he stepped inside. "But some of your neighbors are. And all the lines are connected, see? Your connection's probably in your basement. I need to make sure you're not part of the problem."

"Now? This really isn't a good time." Liz felt compelled to state the obvious.

"Yes, ma'am. I can see that. I'm sorry for the bother. It won't take a minute. If you could show me where . . ."

"Oh, all right," Liz grumbled, and led him to the basement door. She had used up all of her bravado on that ridiculous pose and wasted the effort on the man from the phone company. With any luck she'd get rid of him in no time and be ready to try again when Evan arrived.

He lumbered behind her like an obedient dog down the basement steps and located the telephone wiring in no time. Liz watched in silence while he connected his big orange portable phone to the jack and dialed some numbers. She rubbed her arms against the chill, and prayed her dress wouldn't pick up dust bunnies.

He removed the cigar from his mouth and grinned. There was a huge gap between his tobacco-stained front teeth. "All clear. You're not part of the problem," he told her.

"I'm thrilled, believe me, to be part of the solution," Liz commented as she led the way back up the stairs. They rounded the corner at the top and Liz nearly fell back on top of him as the strap of her dress caught on a coat hook near the door. Liz cried out and he bumped into her, propelling her forward. The unmistakable sound of ripping fabric followed.

"Oh, no! My dress!" Horrified, Liz clutched the bodice to her bosom with one hand and examined the broken strap with the other.

Curly had the good grace to look abashed. "Sorry about that, ma'am."

"Oh, no. What am I going to do!" Liz glanced at the clock. Evan would be here any second. "Come here." She grabbed his beefy hand. "You have to help me." She pulled him along in her wake, his tools and phone dangling from his belt.

"Oh. Oh, no, ma'am, I can't . . ." He dug in his heels at the bedroom door.

"You can and you will," Liz insisted. "It's your fault my strap is ripped. Do you want to be part of the problem or part of the solution?" Frantically she searched through a small box on her dresser for a safety pin.

"Oh, ma'am, please don't ask me to—I'm not good

with ladies' clothes and such." He blushed furiously at the suggestion that he would have to perform such an intimate act. "The phone company will pay for any damage, I'm sure."

"I don't need money," Liz said, voice raised. "I need my dress fixed. Now. And you're going to do it."

She handed him the pin. "See where the strap ripped out there? You pin it so the metal doesn't show from the outside. There's a seam, right? Do the best you can."

When he hesitated, Liz dragged him into the room beneath the light. "Hurry. We don't have much time. He'll be here any minute!"

Evan paused at the partially open front door. *Strange,* he thought, *Why would Liz leave her door open?* Cautiously he stepped inside, tapping on the door as he did so. "Liz?" he called. He laid the bouquet of fresh cut fall flowers on the table and entered the room. Everything appeared normal. Was this some sort of game she was playing? Perhaps she was lying in wait for him. Maybe she had missed him and had a special pre-party surprise for him. "Liz?" he tried again. No answer. Were voices coming from down the hallway?

Evan cocked his head, listening intently. *Just do the best you can. Do it. We don't have much time. He'll be here any minute!* Evan recognized Liz's voice. But who was she talking to?

He gained the door to her bedroom and peered inside. A burly man was bent over Liz's shoulder from behind. There was a two-inch gap between the bottom of the man's shirt and the top of his tool-belt. Evan could barely see the top of Liz's head from where he stood. *What was going on?*

"Liz?" He questioned.

Liz and the man whirled, looking around at the same time as though caught in the act. "Evan!" Liz sounded surprised to see him. Surely she hadn't forgotten their date?

"Am I interrupting something?"

"No, uh—no. Just a minor problem."

"There. All done." Curly stepped back as though extremely proud of himself.

"Thanks, you're a genius. It doesn't even show." Evan's eyebrows rose another notch, while Liz glanced over her shoulder at the mirror behind her.

"No problem. That was easier than I thought it would be. Well, I guess my work here is done." He nodded at Evan. "See ya."

Evan leaned against the doorjamb, arms crossed over his chest. He nodded his chin in the direction he had taken before turning back to her. "He seems like a nice guy."

Liz bit her lip, considering how the scene must have looked to Evan. "Evan, would you do me a favor? Would you go out and come in again, so I can get it right this time?"

Liz waited until she heard the front door close, then checked herself front and back in the mirror. The torn strap was not even noticeable. The doorbell pealed.

"Yes?" she asked as she looked out the tiny window in the door to see Evan.

"It's your lift, Cinderella."

"Please, come in," she said, holding the door open, not bothering to strike any of the poses she'd practiced earlier.

He paused for a moment on the step. Evan Delaford was dumbstruck. Even though he had already seen her in the bedroom, he must not have really noticed the way she looked. The man infamous for being in absolute control of every situation was at a loss.

"You look . . . you look . . ."

Liz raised an eyebrow and smiled. "Yes?"

He raised one of her hands over her head and twirled her around. "Wow!" His heartfelt admiration came through with that simple three-letter word.

"Thanks," she said with a grin. Evan's reaction was even better than she imagined. "And you look divine," she told him pointedly.

For a moment the two of them stood there, poised on the edge of their reactions. "I don't want to mess you up or anything, but—" Evan swooped down before she could react and kissed her. True to his word, he was careful. His hands cupped her head with a light touch. Liz's arms slid around his neck while she eagerly responded. Blood rushed through his veins. He had never felt more alive.

"Wow," she whispered, echoing his earlier response as he ended the kiss.

He couldn't help smiling at her. "I brought you

some flowers." He nodded to the table where he'd left them earlier.

"Thanks." She disengaged herself from his embrace and picked up the bouquet. "These are beautiful. Let me put them in water before we go."

He strolled into the kitchen behind her, glancing around as she filled a vase with water. "So, are you and he . . . close?"

Liz peered at him over the flowers she was busily arranging. "He works for the phone company," she pointed out.

"That much was obvious. Was he wiring you for sound?"

Liz's tinkling laughter sent Evan's spirits soaring. "He had to check the phone lines. The strap of my dress ripped, and he was kind enough to help me fix it. Tell me you didn't think there was anything else going on." She fixed him with a look of pure astonishment and Evan grinned.

"With you, Liz, I'm afraid to hazard a guess. You've described the kind of man you're attracted to, and he definitely falls into that category, don't you think?"

Liz chuckled. Evan had her number, and she didn't mind at all. In fact, she was happy to play along. "He did seem like quite a guy, but apparently he smokes. Not only that, he smokes *cigars*." She shook her head to indicate that he wouldn't make the cut.

"Ah, smoking. When did you add that to the rule-book?

"I meant to tell you the other night how much I like

your house," he commented, glancing around and forcing a change of subject.

"Thank you," she said as she arranged the blooms. "All of the houses along here are tiny. I always imagine Snow White and the Seven Dwarves living in the neighborhood. I think they were all built originally as summer cottages. It's a quiet neighborhood."

"There's a stream out back, I noticed."

"Yes, right behind the retaining wall by my side garden. I have room to park two cars."

"What's it like in the winter?"

She rolled her eyes. "Ah, the snow. Since I don't have a garage, sometimes I get buried. But I also have my cross-country skis, and I'm only a few blocks from work. To tell you the truth," she said in a conspiratorial tone, "I don't mind at all being snowed in. I light a fire and make some soup, and catch up on all the reading I've neglected."

"So Cinderella wasn't far off," he said.

"What?"

"It's a fairy-tale cottage. And you are the beautiful princess."

For just a moment, the silence was awesome. As if hypnotized, she stared into the depths of his compelling blue eyes.

He was the one to break the spell. "Are you about done? We should get going."

"I guess so," she replied, finishing the flower arrangement. "Let me just touch up my lipstick."

* * *

Parked directly in front of her house was a long black limousine, complete with uniformed driver.

"A limousine? Is it going to turn into a pumpkin at midnight?"

He grinned at her surprise. "Well, I thought a limo would be appropriate. You *are* receiving an award, after all. All the winners get out of limos. Don't you watch the Oscars?"

"This is a little different, Evan."

"Only the venue. You're receiving an award from your peers. It's the same thing." He handed her into the car, where she sank into the leather seat.

"We don't have very far to go," she said, a little disappointed the ride would end so quickly.

He bent towards her, and she shivered as she felt his lips next to her ear and his warm breath on her neck. "We'll take the long way home."

Chapter Fourteen

"Oh, stop here!" Liz nearly shouted as the limousine approached a discount store along the way. At Evan's puzzled look, Liz held up her mangled thumbnail. "I almost forgot—I had a slight mishap with my bathroom drawer earlier. I have to fix this."

Evan trailed her through the cosmetics department. Liz had the sinking feeling Evan found her highly amusing in spite of her attempts to impress him with her sophistication. Be that as it may, she desperately wanted to repair her damaged manicure, and he would just have to help her.

To his credit, Evan took it all in stride. He studied the various shades of nail polish she held out to him and helped her choose the closest match. He didn't seem to mind when she borrowed money from him to pay for the polish and a package of emery boards. It hadn't occurred to her to bring any money other than change for an emergency phone call in her evening bag.

They weren't too terribly late, thank goodness, because Liz experienced a sudden attack of nerves as they entered the hotel lobby. Whether it was due to the appreciative glances Evan directed her way during their ride, or because she knew in a few hours she'd have to accept her award in front of hundreds of people, she didn't know. In either case, she excused herself to the ladies' room for a moment alone. Or almost alone.

The only other occupant in the lushly appointed lounge was a blond in a turquoise sequined gown. For some reason the woman looked vaguely familiar to Liz, though surely if she'd ever met such a Barbie doll look-alike, she'd remember. The woman raised a frankly appraising eyebrow at Liz in the mirror. "Nice dress," she commented as she expertly lined her already perfectly made-up lips.

"Thanks," Liz responded. Her stomach was in turmoil. What had she done? she wondered. She had let Evan see the "real" her. Not the mousy librarian with the too-big clothes and oversized glasses. Oh, no, she had gone all out tonight, with the form-fitting Vera Wang, the hair piled in cascading curls on top of her head. Even wore her contacts.

She studied herself in the mirror over the vanity, trying to see what it was Evan saw. All she saw was a passably pretty thirty-something brunette. The dress emphasized her bustline, her height, and her slender

build. *That's why I splurged on it,* she reminded herself. This dress flattered her natural assets. Assets she
had hidden for a very good reason. Longingly, she
thought of her beloved gray sweater. Though Evan had
been nothing but a gentleman thus far, he wasn't totally successful in hiding his interest in her. His bright
blue eyes seem to brand her each time he glanced her
way. Business proposition, indeed!

She snapped open her evening bag and fumbled for
her comb and lipstick, managing to spill virtually
every item onto the counter in the process.

"Take it easy there, hon," the blond said as she
fluffed out her voluminous hair. "This isn't the Acad-
emy Awards, you know."

Liz smiled weakly at her in the mirror. "I know, but
it feels like it to me."

"Yeah, I can see. You're a nervous wreck."

Liz tried to laugh. "It's the guy I'm with. We're
supposed to be just friends, but the way he's been
looking at me . . ." she touched up her lips. What was
she doing discussing Evan with a complete stranger in
a hotel restroom?

The blond laughed. "Honey, I don't care what line
he's been feeding you, they never want to be 'just
friends'."

"I guess it's true," Liz commented, rearranging a
few wisps of her own hair. "Men and women really
can't be friends."

"I don't know." The blond leaned a hip against the
counter and turned toward Liz. "This one guy I dated,
that's all he seemed to want from me. He kept telling

me I wasn't his type." She glanced at herself in the mirror and shook her head. "How could I not be his type?" she asked aloud, though whether she was asking herself or Liz, Liz wasn't sure. "I hung in there for months with him, certain I could bring him around. He was a classy guy. He gave me this when we broke up." She extended her arm to show off a diamond bracelet for Liz to admire.

Liz tucked her things back into her purse and prepared to leave. "I'm sure when it's the right man, you'll know."

The blond nodded. "Yeah, well, I still think *he's* the right one. He'll be back, when he realizes what he gave up."

Evan made his way outside for a breath of fresh air. He needed a moment. Maybe two. Anything to bring him to his senses and keep him from sweeping Liz off her feet when she emerged from the ladies' room.

He had to keep his distance from Liz. She looked sensational, as he knew she would all along once she dropped the Mrs. Doubtfire act. But it wasn't about *how* she looked, though he much preferred the elegantly clad Liz to the dowdy one. Evan found himself more fascinated with what lay beneath the surface. Her heart, her soul. The quirky way she fought her attraction to him. Business proposition indeed! His relationship with Liz had been personal from the start, whether Liz believed it or not. He'd get through the evening, he told himself. Be the perfect gentleman, an undemanding escort. And then he and Liz would settle a few things between them.

"Evan, I've heard so much about you. It's nice to finally meet you." Vivian gave him a glance of approval, and Evan sensed no deceit in her manner. In truth, although they had spoken on one previous occasion, they never had been formally introduced.

"Likewise, I'm sure," Evan said. "I see where Liz gets her good looks."

Vivian's response was lost as Liz's fingers dug into his arm. "Oh, no, please, not this table."

He glanced down to see Liz's gaze fixed on a striking couple making their way toward them. "What is it?" Evan whispered, but it was too late.

"Liz!" The man exclaimed, as though he was just as horrified as Liz at the thought of sharing the table.

"Randy," she returned coolly, her eyes flickering over the woman by his side.

Evan noticed the undercurrents flowing between them.

"You remember Sherry?" He said it in such a way that it was clear he knew Liz couldn't have forgotten.

"Of course." Liz's tone was like ice water. She forced herself to face the woman clad in turquoise and sequins, and faked an enthusiastic smile. "How are you, Sherry?"

The woman murmured something unintelligible. Evan nudged Liz and she dutifully thawed.

"I'm sorry. Randy, this is Evan Delaford. Evan, Randy Hollander, and Sherry . . . ?"

"Walton," they both responded at once, as Randy and Evan shook hands.

Evan had no desire to pursue small talk as his gaze traveled past the couple before him. "Oh, no," he murmured.

"Evan! Sweetheart!" Aileen Summers squealed as she approached, neatly edging Sherry Walton out of the way. Her hands cupped Evan's face and she kissed him square on the lips before he could react. "I had no idea you'd be here!" she told him in delight, as though his presence was a surprise he purposely arranged for her benefit.

"Same here," he said, without the enthusiasm.

"You know Henry Mills, don't you?" she inquired.

"Certainly," Evan acknowledged. "Senator." He shook hands with the other man, then performed introductions, not missing Aileen's appraisal of Liz, nor Liz's stiff countenance. When he turned to complete the introductions to Randy Hollander and Sherry Walton, it was painfully obvious to all present that Sherry and Aileen were dressed nearly identically. The turquoise and sequined cocktail length dresses were obviously products of the same designer. Only a slight difference in the necklines and sleeve lengths kept them from being exactly alike.

"I see we both have excellent taste," Aileen commented dryly, clearly unhappy with her competition.

"Yes," Sherry responded. "Although I wear a size four."

Evan tuned out the rest of their dialogue. As far as he was concerned, not only were their dresses a near match, the two women were cut from the same cloth as well. Next to them, Liz was a breath of fresh air. From her classically cut dress to her hair piled loosely on top of her head, to the delicately applied cosmetics, she was elegantly understated. Her confidence and sense of style radiated from the person beneath the surface, setting her apart from women like Aileen and Sherry. She took his breath away. Undercurrents indeed, Evan told himself, clearing his throat. "Let's sit, shall we?" he suggested, thinking that would give them all time to regroup. Unfortunately his plan backfired.

Aileen piped up in the confident, take-charge tone that had won her a spot on Chicago's highest rated morning news show. "Let's sit boy/girl/boy/girl, and no one sits next to the person they came with. That's always fun, and a great way to meet new people!"

"Aileen," Evan tried. "I don't think—"

"Yes, *let's,*" Liz interrupted. "It will give us a chance to renew old acquaintances." The look she gave Evan was full of meaning, but not one he could interpret, and his hopes for the evening began to disintegrate.

They all did a mad dance around the table, trying to conform to Aileen's configuration. By the time the dust settled, Evan found himself wedged between Aileen and Sherry Walton. Liz sat directly across from him, hemmed in with Senator Mills on one side and Judge Kramer, her mother's date, on the other. Both men attempted to engage her attention, but her eyes darted continually in Evan's direction.

Was this some kind of test? Evan wondered. Was she waiting to see what effect being seated next to his former girlfriend had on him? None at all, he wanted to tell her. He'd much rather sit next to Liz, that was for sure. He shook his head the next time he caught her eye, a silent message to convey he had no interest in Aileen Summers.

A quick glance around the table confirmed his suspicion. Aileen was the only one truly happy with the seating arrangement. Good manners, however, prevented anyone from objecting. This promised to be a very long evening.

The appetizer was served and the meal progressed. The uncomfortable seating arrangement became nearly intolerable.

Sherry received numerous derisive glances from Aileen each time she engaged Evan in conversation. While Sherry prattled, Aileen turned her attention to Randy in retaliation.

"So, Randy, why don't you tell me all about yourself? Property and casualty insurance must be a fascinating field."

Evan tuned out both women and watched in amusement as Vivian and Judge Kramer shot knowing glances at each other across the table, and winked conspiratorially when they thought no one was looking.

If he could have, Evan would have suggested to Liz that they leave, but that was impossible. So he endured Sherry's endless chatter on his left and Aileen's attempts to make him jealous by flirting with Randy on his right. The announcement for the awards ceremony came none too soon. He watched the Senator glad-hand his way to the podium, and listened with half an ear while the man ran through his brief speech.

Liz repositioned her chair to better see the stage, and Evan gazed at her profile. His thoughts drifted to his first glimpse of her, a few short weeks ago. She had intrigued him then, the wisps of dark hair curling around her face, the delicate curve of her jaw. He was even more captivated by her now. He wanted to delve into her mind, discover the secrets she hid from the rest of the world and why. He wanted to know what made her tick, what pushed those contrary buttons of hers. And he would, he promised himself, as he watched her weave gracefully through the maze of ta-bles to the stage and accept her award from Aileen.

When the applause died down, Liz licked her lips nervously and spoke into the microphone, her voice sincere. "I really didn't do anything special to win this award," she began. "I did what needed to be done. Our children are our future, and I think sometimes we forget that. If we raise an illiterate generation, we au-tomatically lower standards for not only our future, but theirs as well.

"I've always believed that a child who learns to read can learn to do anything. And if the literacy campaign helps even one child to understand that, then it's a worthwhile cause. I ask each and every one of you to think about not only the future of our children, but the future of our country, and to support the literacy volunteers in your area. I promise you, you won't regret it. Thank you."

A thunder of applause followed her remarks, and a standing ovation ensued as she made her way back to the table. Evan wanted to sweep her up in his arms and tell her how proud he was of her, but he was prevented from doing that. Vivian got to her first and was followed by Judge Kramer. Then numerous other well-wishers crowded around to congratulate her.

Finally, dancing was announced. Liz resumed her seat.

"May I have this dance?" With a twinkle in his eye Evan held out his hand to Liz.

Just as Liz put her hand in his a waiter approached Evan. "Excuse me, sir. Could you come with me for a moment?"

Evan sent Liz a puzzled look. "I'll be right back." He followed the waiter through the double doors.

"You witch!" Sherry hissed at Aileen.

Randy Hollander stood between the two women, an unmistakable trace of lipstick on his chin.

"Uh-oh," Evan said.

"You understand why I asked you to come?" The anxious waiter peered up at Evan.

"I'll take care of it," Evan replied, as the waiter escaped back into the dining room.

So much for my perfect evening, Liz thought. *Having a date hardly guaranteed a happy ending.* She spent most of dinner watching Evan wedged between his stunning former girlfriend and her ex-boyfriend's gorgeous fiancée.

A glance at her watch told her it had been twenty minutes since Evan disappeared.

Vivian and the Judge kept Liz company for a while, but the beat of the live music proved too much for them and they escaped to the dance floor.

Liz would waste no time in pointing out to Vivian the next chance she got that having a suitable escort for the evening didn't translate into a good time.

Besides, it wasn't a real date, she reminded herself. Evan did her a favor because he owed her. Maybe he was interested in her, maybe he wasn't, but did it really matter?

He'd soon return to Chicago, back to his penthouse apartment, his workaholic lifestyle, and whatever beauty queen was next in line. And where would she be? Sitting here in Rockleigh, in her frumpy sweater and her too-big glasses waiting for Prince Charming to charge up and sweep her off her feet. *It's not going to happen,* she told herself, as she absent-mindedly twisted her award round and round on the table in front of her. Her vision blurred with unshed tears. She'd wasted what little time she'd had with Evan playing by her stupid rules, dressing in her ugly clothes, and acting like she didn't care.

"May I have this dance?"

Liz blinked and turned to see a masculine hand outstretched in her direction. She blinked again and looked up to see Evan. This might be her last opportunity to make a lasting impression on him. She put her hand in his and allowed him to lead her to the dance floor.

The band played a near-perfect rendition of an old Temptations hit. Liz allowed herself to relax into Evan's lead while she listened to the lyrics.

"Is everything all right?" Liz asked softly. The scent of Evan's subtle, spicy cologne swirled around her. Her knees went weak and her brain turned to mush. What she wanted to do was lay her head on Evan's shoulder and snuggle up against him and let him hold her close.

"Everything's fine," he murmured. He brushed his lips against her temple and pulled her closer. Liz closed her eyes. At that moment, she could almost believe in fairy tales—and in Prince Charming.

"Would you like to go home?" he asked.

Liz nodded, reluctantly opening her eyes. *Anywhere,* she answered him silently. *Anywhere as long as it's with you.*

Chapter Fifteen

"It was quite a mess," Evan answered in reply to Liz's question about what ensued once he left the ballroom. "Sherry was nearly hysterical, and it only got worse. I sent Aileen into the ladies' room, and I almost had Sherry calmed down when Randy attempted to explain." Evan shook his head. "You'd think he'd have sense enough to wipe Aileen's lipstick off of his face before that, but he didn't."

"He probably didn't even know it was there," Liz put in. *Vintage Randy,* she thought, *oblivious to everything but his own pleasure.*

"Probably not," Evan agreed. "But it was like waving a red flag in front of Sherry. The woman went ballistic. Which reminds me," Evan raised an eyebrow as he turned to her. "Your distress over having them at our table was obvious, but I never got a chance to ask you why."

A laugh bubbled in her throat, and Liz nearly choked on it. Admitting to Evan that she was once involved with Randy Hollander would be like throwing gasoline on a raging fire. She could just see her rule book going up in smoke in the face of such overwhelming evidence, contrary to everything she'd told him.

"What?" Evan's eyes were alight with interest.

After the evening she had just put him through, she certainly owed him an explanation. "I used to date Randy." There. Simple. Direct. She wanted to look out the window, but the dark tinted glass threw her reflection back at her and she saw Evan watching her intently over her shoulder.

"You dated him? Seriously?"

"Did I seriously date him? Or am I being serious when I tell you that I did? Never mind. I dated him—seriously."

"A good-looking guy like that. Huh!" Evan sat back to contemplate this revelation in silence.

"Until he met Sherry." Liz offered this further information into the gloom in the back of the limo.

Evan turned to her once again. "He dumped *you* for *her?*"

His incredulity was lost on Liz. She laid her head back against the plush leather seat and closed her eyes. "I should have known better," she told him quietly.

"My instincts for self-preservation have improved quite a bit since then."

"He hurt you," Evan stated.

Liz opened her eyes, surprised and touched to see the fierce protectiveness in Evan's gaze. She gave him a tiny smile and a shrug before closing her eyes again. "As I said, I should have known better."

Evan slid his hand beneath hers on the seat next to them and linked their fingers together. A warm tingle rushed through Liz and she caught her breath, trying to act as though his touch had no effect. "What about Aileen?" she asked shakily. A neat change of subject. Perhaps it would cool things down for Evan to talk about his ex.

She felt him relax back on the seat next to her, his shoulder brushing hers. A low rumbling chuckle preceded his words. "Poor Aileen. I don't think I've ever seen her looking quite so bedraggled. Once I managed to get Sherry and Randy into a cab and came back inside, Senator Mills was passed out in the lobby. Aileen's dress was ripped, so the concierge brought her one of the hotel bathrobes to cover up."

In spite of herself, Liz giggled at the image. It really wasn't fair of her and Evan to have a good laugh at the expense of the other woman.

"I guess the heel of her shoe must have broken off, because she was barefoot when she came out of the restroom, trailing sequins in her wake," Evan said.

"Oh, Evan, no," Liz laughed.

"One of her eyelashes was coming unglued, but at the time, I saw no need to mention it to her."

Liz shrieked with laughter.

"Did I tell you several of her hair extensions were apparently lost in the scuffle? I suspect she might be a candidate for hair replacement."

"Evan, stop!" Liz was nearly hysterical.

"No, seriously, the last thing I saw was her tending to poor Senator Mills in the hotel lobby, while several of the hotel staff attempted to revive him. Luckily, there were only a couple of local reporters and photographers on the scene since it was so late. I'm sure there won't be much of a story."

"Oh, poor Aileen!" Liz's laughter abruptly died. Even though the woman was Evan's ex-girlfriend, Liz couldn't be happy about Aileen's fate this evening.

Evan squeezed Liz's hand. "Trust me, Liz. No matter what the headlines read, Aileen will put a positive spin on it. Don't be surprised if she comes out the heroine. *Ex-Miss Illinois Saves Senator's Life Using Mouth-to-Mouth Resuscitation.*"

"She can do that? Twist things around that way?"

Evan's grin was slightly bitter. "She can, and she will. I ought to know. She manipulated the press every which way when she and I dated. I'm still surprised there was never a formal engagement announcement."

"Did you propose?" Liz knew it was none of her business, but in truth, she was dying to know.

"Uh-uh. No way, no how. Aileen is not the type of woman I could ever be serious about." Evan was so adamant that Liz believed him.

"Why not?" she asked softly. They had both sunk

comfortably down into the plush seat, their heads turned toward each other as they talked.

"Aileen has no depth." Evan's voice was quiet, matter of fact. "She's like a fireworks display. An exciting flash which lasts only a short time. There's nothing underneath. Nothing to sustain *my* interest, anyway." He reached out and ran his forefinger along Liz's jaw. Liz felt her heart thud in her chest. He was going to kiss her again.

The limousine eased into a parking place in front of Liz's house and stopped. The driver hopped out and opened the door. The moment was gone.

"Thank you for helping out this evening, Evan." Liz did her best to pretend she didn't long for him to kiss her.

Evan turned his attention from glowering at the driver who was oblivious to his passenger's consternation. "It was my pleasure, and I think you know that."

Liz rewarded him with a smile. "Can I offer you the added bonus of coming in for coffee, then?"

Evan was out of the car in a flash. He held out a hand to her while the chauffeur stood stiffly behind him. As they walked to the door, he tried to remember the last time it took a woman so long to invite him in for coffee.

While Liz made coffee in the kitchen, Evan prowled the cozy living room. Liz's filled bookshelves rivaled his own with their store of classic literature and recent bestsellers. Like himself, Liz apparently had eclectic tastes in her reading material. He noted titles ranging from whimsical to neo-political, along with numerous children's favorites.

What else had he not guessed about Liz Brady? he wondered. He was right in his first estimation that beneath the dowdy exterior lurked a beautiful woman with a warm heart and a passion for life. How fascinating it would be to spend the rest of his life finding out every minute detail which made up Liz Brady, Rockleigh County Librarian and master of disguise.

"Here we are," Liz said, as she entered the room bearing a tray with a coffeepot and all the necessary accouterments. "I have cookies, too, if you'd like," she offered.

Evan poured coffee for them both before joining her on the deeply cushioned sofa. Now that they were alone, it seemed neither of them could think of anything to say. They sipped their coffee while offering each other skittish eye contact and weak smiles. The huge question *now what?* loomed between them.

Evan set his cup down on the table, and in an unaccustomed nervous gesture, wiped damp palms down his pants legs. He couldn't stand this any longer. He turned to Liz.

"You look—"

"I was just—"

They both stopped abruptly, and for the first time their eyes met and held. Evan did something he'd wanted to do all evening. Stretching an arm along the back of the sofa, he wound a wisp of Liz's hair around his index finger. His gaze moved to the strand of hair he captured, then back to her face. "You look lovely tonight." Before Liz could take offense at the compliment, he waylaid her objection. "Not that you don't always look lovely. But you look . . . especially beautiful tonight."

Was his voice hesitating? Had he faltered over the words? Compliments to women dripped off Evan's tongue since adolescence. Why was it that now, with Liz Brady, he could barely think straight, much less speak, at a time he most wanted to impress her?

Her green eyes were luminous, and she gave him a tremulous smile as her hand came up to wrap around his. "Thank you, Evan," she answered softly.

Slowly, ever so slowly, his fingers wound their way through her dark hair. Inch by agonizing inch he drew her to him as he leaned toward her, until their lips met in a sweet touch.

Evan continued to touch Liz's lips lightly with his own. Nothing about Liz was as it should have been from the beginning; maybe because she'd fought her attraction to him from the moment they'd met. He suddenly envisioned endless days and weeks and months with Liz. Years down the road he would discover some unknown yet wonderful facet of her personality. *There's no need to hurry.*

Liz's lips met his. He was drowning, awash in her perfume, the feel of her hair and skin beneath his fingertips. He forgot about questions and answers and time stood still.

He stood and drew her up, holding both her hands, bringing her close to him.

He kissed her breathless before letting her go. He

whispered, "Are you sure you're ready to break that policy of yours about getting involved with good-looking men?"

He heard Liz chuckle low in her throat. "Yes, I'm sure. But I'm really glad I didn't break my other policy. Otherwise I'd have shared this evening with Kenny."

He tightened his hold on her.

"And I *wouldn't* have invited him in for coffee," Liz whispered.

Evan groaned. Her other policy. Her other hard-and-fast policy about not dating men her mother set her up with. But unbeknownst to Liz, Vivian Brady *was* responsible for his being here! *Would she see the humor in it now?* he wondered as he tried to decide what to do.

He seared her lips with another kiss, hoping to distract her before he whispered, "What if your mother had arranged for us to meet?"

Evan felt Liz's smile beneath his lips. "That's silly," she mumbled between kisses. "My mother didn't set us up."

"But what if she did?" The question hung between them while Evan continued kissing her.

"But she didn't," Liz pointed out.

When he didn't immediately agree with her last statement, Liz stilled. He gazed down into her troubled eyes. "Evan, why would you ask me that now?"

Liz was not amused.

Evan muttered a mild curse.

That one word, uttered by Evan in such a tone of resignation, sent warning bells off in Liz's brain.

"Evan?" Liz hated the pleading tone she heard in her own voice.

Evan's expression was regretful, almost apologetic, and Liz felt her heart sink.

"Evan, please tell me you never met my mother before tonight?"

When he didn't answer, Liz covered her mouth with her hands. "My mother didn't find you through a personal ad!" Liz was incredulous.

A corner of Evan's mouth lifted in a sad smile. "Not exactly."

"But my mother *did* set us up?" She had to be sure. She wanted to understand. Because if Evan Delaford was going to break her heart, she wanted to know the truth.

"Not exactly. She made a mistake . . ."

Evan stalled for time, but if he didn't come clean with her pretty soon, it wasn't going to make any difference. Based on the awful suspicions forming in Liz's mind, it might not make any difference anyway.

"Did my mother arrange for us to meet?" Liz kept her voice as steady as possible under the circumstances. Vivian set her up, and apparently Evan played along all this time.

"Liz, it wasn't like that. It was a mistake," Evan tried again. By the time he got the words out, Liz had backed away from him.

"You keep saying it was a mistake!" Liz exploded. "Well, apparently I'm the only one who made a mistake. About you. I knew better. I *knew,* and I still fell for you!" she shouted, barely aware of what she'd just admitted.

"Liz—" Evan tried to take her hands in his, calm her down, but she shook him off.

"No! You stay away from me, Mr. Charm. You knew all along how I felt about my mother and her set-ups, and yet you were in on it the whole time. You used me!" she cried. "You made me like you, you made me trust you just so you could make a fool of me—"

"Liz, that's not true!" Evan exploded. He advanced on her again, wanting to make her understand, but she backed further away.

"Don't touch me! Don't even try!" She darted behind a chair, using it as a barrier to put distance between herself and Evan. "This was all just a game to you, wasn't it?" she asked, as if she'd finally found the last piece to a puzzle she'd been working on for years.

"It wasn't a game." Evan's voice was icy calm, his eyes so dark and intense she almost believed him. But she couldn't. Not now.

"Oh, really?" Liz bit out the challenge. "Then what do you call it when your initial offer of dinner was for 'strictly business' purposes?" Her words echoed around the room in a high mimicking tone. "I bet you knew then I had an aversion to dating good-looking guys like you, because my mother would have told you."

The guilty look on Evan's face confirmed she'd been right all along.

"So instead of asking me out because you knew I'd turn you down for a 'date', you give me this song-and-dance about helping you with your research." Liz purposely chose to overlook the fact that part of Evan's story was true: he *was* in Rockleigh on business, and checking out the Goodtimes restaurant chain was a big part of it. "And then when you try to take it to a personal level, and I tell you no, you do that stupid bit with the jeans and the T-shirt." Liz bit her lip, because Evan's effort had really touched her heart. It was one of the things which made her believe he was truly interested in her. He went to so much trouble to be what she claimed she wanted. She still had a vivid recollection of Evan's rough-and-tumble appearance, even as he stood not ten feet from her in his expensive evening clothes.

"So all this time you spent wearing me down, playing with me—"

"I wasn't playing," Evan interrupted. "And neither were you," he informed her coldly.

Tears welled in her eyes, but she refused to let them fall. "No, I wasn't," she agreed. She lifted her chin. "But what else haven't you told me? Do you have the current Miss Illinois stashed back home in Chicago? Or is it Miss Ohio this month?" she added sarcastically.

"Liz, let me explain."

"You know what I never could figure out?" she asked, as though he hadn't spoken. "Why you even bothered with me, when you could have your pick. Why settle for plain old Venetian blinds when you can have brocade velvet draperies?"

"Liz, you've got this all wrong. It's not like—"

"You know what, Evan? I no longer have an aversion to dating good-looking men. But I've suddenly developed an aversion to you."

"Liz, please—"

"Get out."

"Just listen to me," Evan insisted.

"Get out!" Liz shouted. "Get out now or I'll make you regret it." If he didn't leave right this minute, she'd make a fool of herself in front of him. He'd wear her down, make her let him explain everything. She'd probably fall right into his arms and believe every word he said.

Her determined attitude must have convinced him. Evan yanked on his coat and stalked to the door before turning back to her. "Liz, this isn't what it seems."

"No." Liz shook her head sadly. "Nothing ever is."

Chapter Sixteen

W hat should have been one of the best evenings of Liz's life faded into nothing but bad memories. Why hadn't she seen it coming? Had Evan so captivated her she'd ignored all the warning signs?

By morning her sense of outrage was second only to the embarrassment which streaked up and down her spine each time she replayed Evan's confession in her mind. She wanted to climb right back into her bed and hide. Oh! And to think she went out of her way to make herself look beautiful for him. *For him!*

He must be proud of himself, she thought. Evan knew her rules, and had managed to break through every one, yet harbor no guilt because he'd confessed. It must have been a very entertaining three weeks for him. A novel experience, so different from his sophisticated day-to-day existence, where the only rules he played by were his own.

If she didn't get rid of all of this anger she'd explode. What was done was done. She needed to move forward, the sooner the better. It did no good to take it out on herself. She pulled on her running shoes and sweats.

She jogged out the front door. She could do five miles instead of three. An extra long run would make her feel better and get the anger and hurt out of her system.

How could he be so stupid? Evan mentally kicked himself at least twenty times since the fiasco of the evening before. He'd tossed and turned all night, berating himself for telling Liz of Vivian's role in their meeting. He knew her feelings on the subject, and the silly rules of her love life. He never imagined she would turn him away on a technicality, just when she seemed to be allowing him into her life.

Evan Delaford never lost. He didn't know how. He always managed to pull a deal together, even if it was at the last moment. People *wanted* to please him, to work with him, to let him make things right. He had earned the nickname "Magician" in the business world for all the proverbial deals he pulled out of his hat. He possessed an uncanny ability to compromise, to find a solution that would please all parties. Matters of the heart were not unlike business. But being good at one certainly did not make him a master at the other.

He couldn't believe he now stood to lose the most important deal of his life.

Evan felt hollow inside when he thought how Liz wanted no part of him. Liz held all the winning cards and he had none. Except he loved her. His ace in the hole. Evan Delaford would not go down without a fight.

Liz now ranked him with the lowest of the low. Why? Because he told her the truth? No. Because he waited until he *had* to tell her the truth. He overlooked one crucial detail: his confession did not necessarily guarantee her forgiveness. There was no benefit in telling her the truth in order to ease his conscience. He wanted to go into the deal feeling clean, with no deceit between them. His misguided honesty should, at the very least, make him feel better. But how could it, when all he managed to do was destroy the tenuous relationship he'd worked so hard to build?

It was wrong to ever have deceived Liz in the first place, he admitted, but how was he to know she really meant what she said? Women, at least in his experience, meant only about half of what came out of their mouths.

He never cared enough before now to figure out which half was meant.

His palms were sweating when he picked up the phone to call her. He replaced it and took a couple of deep breaths, wiping his hands on his slacks. Rehearsing in his head what he would say, he picked up the phone again and then dropped it back in the cradle. Should he start with an apology? He certainly regretted the way things turned out last night, but he wasn't about to grovel, either. *Come on, Evan old man,* he cajoled himself. *It isn't like this is the deal of the century.* No, he thought, *just the most important deal of my life.*

He held his breath and dialed her number. After four rings, her answering machine picked up. He listened to her recorded voice instructing him to leave a message. After the beep, he contemplated hanging up. Instead he plunged in.

"Liz, this is Evan. I need to talk to you. Please call me when you come in." There. Simple. Straightforward. He could apologize when he saw her. When she called. *If* she called.

Looking out his hotel window, he watched as several runners jogged along the path overlooking the small lake. *Exercise might help,* he thought. *Run a few miles and get it out of my system.* He pulled on a sweatshirt and some shorts, and headed down to the running path. The feel of the wind in his face would help clear his head and give him some ideas on what to say when and if Liz called him back.

Liz ran less than a mile before she found herself in front of her mother's house, breathing in deep gulps of air. *I wonder,* thought Liz, *if she even realizes what she did? Does she ever take me seriously, or does she still think of me as her little girl?*

Liz let herself in the gate and walked up to the front door, with its bright, seasonal wreath welcoming visitors to the house. She never went in the front door.

In the kitchen she found her mother, looking well-rested and composed.

"Good morning, dear. What a lovely surprise. Would you care for some breakfast?"

"No, I'm not really hungry," said Liz. "I'll have some coffee and a word with you, if you have the time."

"My, how formal that sounds. Are you upset about something?" Vivian asked, as she poured coffee and set it before Liz, who had assumed her old seat at the breakfast table.

"You might say so. You never told me, Mom," she paused to sip the coffee and to build up the necessary nerve she needed to confront her mother, "that you set me up with Evan, and that you had met him before I did. He never would have given me a second glance if not for your interference. I never would have met him if not for you."

Vivian took her seat opposite Liz and seemed to consider how to deal with Liz's statements. Apparently a number of things rolled through her mind, as Liz watched her consider and then mentally discard a couple of responses.

"That's right. Without my 'interference' as you call it, you never would have met him," Vivian answered quietly, completely calm and sure of herself.

"But you *know* how I feel. You know there's no way I'd get involved with anyone you set me up with."

"Liz, I may have been instrumental in you two meeting, but whether or not you choose to become involved with Evan is entirely up to you," Vivian pointed out. "Would you rather go out with a stranger? With someone you just met on the street? Someone you weren't introduced to?"

"No," she replied, not certain of where this was heading. In fact, she had been doing all of those things since meeting Evan.

"Good, I'm glad to hear it. Would you go out with someone from work?"

"No," said Liz, "definitely not," as she mentally pictured the two available male employees, both at least twenty years older than she.

"For goodness sake, Liz! How on earth do you think you'll ever meet anyone? Where do you draw the line between being introduced to a man, and being 'fixed up' with one? Your 'rules' practically guarantee that you'll never meet anyone, anywhere!"

"My rules worked just fine until you interfered," Liz insisted. "And the purpose of *my rules* was to keep me from getting hurt again, Mom. I thought you understood. I really thought you did." How could her mother be so oblivious to her sense of betrayal?

"Maybe you thought you were protecting yourself, Liz, But all I saw was how lonely you were. I did interfere, and I'll apologize if you want me to, but I don't regret what I did. I had already called a man I'd found through the personal ads before I ever talked to you about doing it. That's how I met Evan."

Liz shook her head in denial. "Mom, that's impossible. Evan Delaford was *not* in that restaurant because you set up a meeting with him."

"Of course he was," Vivian insisted. "He was in the

right place at the right time. He had a copy of *The New York Times Book Review* with him. That's how I recognized him."

Liz shook her head. "Mom, I'm telling you, Evan was only in the restaurant because of his business. He wasn't there because of a personal ad."

A lightbulb seemed to flash above Vivian's head as comprehension dawned, and her expression changed to one of confused wonder. "Come to think about it, he did try to tell me he wasn't the person I was looking for."

"And?" Liz prompted.

Vivian had the good grace to blush. "I thought it was because he'd seen you. You were wearing your awful gray sweater and one of those baggy dresses as usual. I told him it was just a phase you were going through—"

"Mother! You didn't." It was even worse than she first thought. Evan hadn't even wanted to approach her. Only her mother's invisible hand at his back pushed him into it.

"Liz, do you know what this means?" Vivian asked excitedly. "Meeting Evan was a fluke, one of those wonderful accidents even *I* couldn't possibly plan, because nothing *ever* goes that well. I didn't set you up with him, I just suggested he speak with you, that's all. He kept glancing at you the whole time I talked to him. Then I remembered your 'rules,' and I told him to forget it."

"You what?"

"One look at his handsome face was all it took for

me to know you would never consider going out with him. He looked like everything a mother could possibly want for her daughter: handsome, neat, obviously successful. Perhaps it was wishful thinking on my part. Evan is all of those things and more."

Vivian took note of Liz's downcast expression and reached across the table to cover one of Liz's hands with her own. "Darling, he insisted on speaking with you, even after I told him it would be a waste of his time."

"Really?" Liz breathed, as hope sprang into her eyes.

"Really," Vivian confirmed. "Sweetheart, I see the way you are when you're with him. You're back to being the Liz we all know and love. I'm sorry life threw you such a bad curve that you chose to block all avenues of meeting eligible young men, but I will *never* be sorry I spoke to Evan Delaford that day in Goodtimes."

Vivian took a deep breath after she finished speaking, her eyes full of affection.

"Liz, you can decide to stop seeing Evan. But don't blame me for your meeting in the first place as the reason. Don't be so stubborn that you win on principle and lose the opportunity life has thrown your way. Some of the best love stories I've ever heard are based on accidental meetings."

The queasy feeling in the pit of her stomach told Liz that Vivian struck more than a few valid points. She had closed herself off, and maybe, just maybe, she went too far in the other direction.

"Thanks for the coffee, Mom. I think I'll head on down to the running path by the lake. I have some thinking to do."

The only thing noteworthy about Evan's run was the pair of golden retrievers bounding along with their master by the lake. Their shiny coats and bright eyes reminded Evan of Casey. It was a sad reflection on his life, he supposed, that after all this time away from Chicago, what he found he missed most was his dog. He ran past Liz's house, and although her car was there, there was no answer when he rang the bell. Trying not to feel too dejected, he headed back to his hotel.

There were no messages when he got back to the room. He sighed as he considered principles. He had a couple of his own he was adamant about, so he grudgingly respected Liz for standing by hers. Now, he thought, if only she could realize that principles could occasionally be set aside!

After a shower and a shave, he tried her number two more times. *One more time,* he thought, as he picked up the phone.

Once again, the machine answered his call. He hoped after the previous four messages her machine didn't run out of tape. Where was she, anyway?

"Liz, this is Evan. I'm sorry for the way things worked out between us last night. If you don't want to talk to me, I understand. I'm heading back to Chicago at three this afternoon." He cleared his throat, recalling the reason why he'd scheduled the return trip for so late in the day. According to his plan, he was to have spent most of today with Liz. Of course, this was before his brilliant plan went up in smoke. "My private line is listed on the card I gave you, and only I answer it.

"Liz, there's something I'd really like to tell you, but I can't say it over the phone, so I wish you'd call me. Take care, Liz. I'll—" he paused for just a fraction of a second, ". . . miss you."

Liz looked at every man with Evan's general proportions on the running path. Could she imagine her life without ever seeing him again? A man in a bright blue running suit trotted by at a fast clip, twin golden retrievers keeping pace. She smiled, thinking of the picture of Evan rough-housing with his dog.

The miles added up. She ran at least four before she staggered back to her house and into the shower.

As she stood under the spray, she thought about everything her mother said. Re-examining how her mother had approached Evan out of the blue, she laughed out loud. *I wish I could have seen his face!* Poor Evan—caught between a rock and a hard place! Her mother was the rock and she supposed that made her the hard place. He tried to break through her defenses and she let him. But when he got too close, she threw yet another boulder in his path and all but kicked him out of her house. She made all the rules, but she certainly hadn't been playing fair.

She was still laughing as she stepped out of the shower, and pulled on jeans and a comfortable form-fitting turtleneck. Gone was the frumpy librarian, and in her place stood a vibrant young woman, flushed from exercise, looking back at her from the mirror. She took a few minutes to blow-dry her hair, leaving it full and soft around her face. Then she applied the barest minimum of make-up to enhance her glowing complexion. "Good-bye," she whispered, as she tucked her glasses into the drawer of her nightstand.

The phone rang, but before she could pick it up the answering machine kicked on. Her mother's voice came over the recorder while she listened, and noticed for the first time that the message light was blinking furiously. "Darling, it's mom. I'm so sorry I hurt your feelings. You take it so personally that you haven't met the perfect man on your own. You have to realize, that's very unusual. Most times, young people are brought together by friends, by family. Some way other than by themselves. Life can't go on in a vacuum.

"If you can't bring yourself to forgive me for interfering, I'll understand, and I promise never, ever to get involved in your personal life again. You have my word. But darling, *please* don't let a perfectly wonderful opportunity for love pass you by because of principle. A principle will not hold you and keep you warm at night."

When her mother hung up, the message light flashed five times. My, my, wasn't she the popular one today. She sat down on the bed with a pad and pencil and replayed the messages.

The first four messages were from Evan. With each

successive message, she heard his voice go from hopeful to resigned. Her heart lurched, and tears welled in her eyes. Was she really willing to say good-bye to Evan Delaford forever?

A tear tracked slowly down her cheek. Grabbing a tissue, she blew her nose and looked at the clock.

It was almost two o'clock! Evan's flight took off at three. She dialed the hotel where he was staying.

"Room 806, please," she said.

"One moment, please," requested the operator.

She waited, hoping she wasn't too late.

"Miss? I'm sorry. Mr. Delaford already checked out."

Checked out! She might not even get to say good-bye to him. He must think her childish for playing games with him, using her silly set of rules. But was she too late to let him know he was more important to her than her misguided dating policies, and that the only important principle was her love for him?

She gathered her purse and keys and hurried out to her car. *Please, please,* she repeated as her mantra, *let me be on time.*

Despite having driven to the airport dozens of times to pick up her sisters over the last couple of years, this particular trip seemed to drag on forever. Every second was torture. As she approached the area where the flight paths were visible from the highway, she watched two commuter flights climb into the clouds, one after the other. Was Evan on one of those planes? Would he disappear into the clouds before she had a chance to tell him how she felt?

She snatched the ticket for short-term parking from the machine and watched the bar rise in slow motion. Several travelers, their luggage trailing behind them, meandered in front of her, blocking her way. "Move, move, move!" she instructed them, though they couldn't hear her. She beeped her horn in agitation, which had the reverse effect of slowing them down even more.

By the time she'd maneuvered around them and parked, panic had set in. What if she missed him? He'd asked her to call before he left the hotel and she hadn't. What if she'd ruined any chance of a future with Evan because of her own misguided thinking and unwillingness to listen?

She sprinted into the terminal and slid to a halt in front of the nearest flight monitor. Only one flight was scheduled for Chicago, at 3:20.

One look at her watch told her they might be boarding already. First class passengers boarded first! She had no doubt Evan flew first class. But they'd never let her on the plane without a ticket. Maybe she could coerce a sympathetic airline attendant to drag Evan off the plane so she could talk to him.

At the gate, only a few passengers lounged nearby. No Evan. She approached the check-in counter. "Excuse me, has your flight to Chicago boarded yet?"

"No ma'am," answered the young clerk. "Not for another few minutes."

"Oh." Deflated, Liz scanned the waiting passengers again. Then she turned and panned the entire area. No sign of Evan. Inspiration struck. She turned back to the clerk.

"My, uh, my husband should be on this flight. Could you tell me if he's checked in yet?"

"Certainly, ma'am. The name?"

"Evan Delaford."

The clerk's fingers flitted across a keyboard. He studied the computer screen in front of him, a frown furrowing between his brows. "Delaford, you said. D-E-L-A-F-O-R-D, right?"

"Yes, that's right. Evan Delaford." *Hurry, hurry, hurry!* Liz silently screamed.

"Hmmm. I don't show an Evan Delaford booked on this flight, ma'am."

Liz's hopes deflated like a burst balloon. "But, but, he's leaving for Chicago at three. This is the only flight listed."

"Yes, ma'am."

"Then where could he be?" Liz wanted to stomp her foot in frustration. In fact, she wanted to do something she hadn't done since the age of three—indulge in a no-holds-barred temper tantrum.

"You might try the civil aviation terminal. Perhaps he's taking a non-commercial flight," the clerk suggested.

"Oh, my goodness! Yes, of course, that's it. Oh, thank you, thank you, thank you!" Evan had mentioned his recent acquisition of a corporate jet during their first dinner together. Liz scooted around the counter and hugged the surprised clerk. She dashed down the corridor before it occurred to her she had no idea where to go. She slid into reverse. The clerk saw her coming.

"Go out the main terminal entrance. Hang a left. It's the big green building on the right."

She waved her thanks and took off.

What if he had already boarded the plane, though? How would she know which plane was his? Would he even let her on board after the way she behaved last night?

She could always call him later, she supposed. Her heart sank at the thought. By then he'd be back in Chicago, and she couldn't envision saying the things she needed to say over the phone. What if she had lost him for good?

The civil air terminal was a smaller version of the main one. Liz frantically scanned the waiting area and saw no one. Where was Evan? She spotted a news-stand and headed for it, praying he'd be there.

Nothing. No Evan. She refused to give in to despair. *He has to be here,* she insisted to the powers that be. *He has to be!*

She peeked around a circular display of books just to make sure. A man stood next to the rack, his back to her. Her heart raced with joy. She'd memorized his dark, slightly too-long hair and broad shoulders. She'd recognize him anywhere.

Evan didn't notice her silent advance. He was studying the back cover blurb on a book with the puzzled expression she had come to know so well. Curiously she glanced down at the book in his hand and smiled. It was that bestseller on male/female relationships, the one that asserts that men and women are unable to communicate because, according to the author, they are essentially living on different planets.

A lump formed in Liz's throat. Poor Evan. He was still trying to figure it all out. Maybe she could help him . . . if it wasn't too late. If he'd give her another chance.

She drew a deep breath and edged closer. "You know, you really have to be careful which book you choose."

She watched his expression change. For a high stakes' gambler, he was very transparent! He turned toward her and her heart soared. His gaze washed lovingly over her.

"Why is that?" he asked. The low timbre of his voice caused her insides to quiver. Had she really considered letting him go?

"Some books are harder to read than others. They take a little more effort, but sometimes it's worth it."

He moved closer and placed the book back in the rack. "Are those the ones that end with 'and they lived happily ever after'?"

Liz smiled. "I've always been partial to happy endings." She studied his face, memorizing every angle as if she'd never get another chance.

"Ah," he said. "You prefer the classics. How do you like this ending: the guy gets the girl and they live happily ever after."

"I would like that more than anything."

"But we'd have to have a few . . . guidelines, wouldn't we?"

"Guidelines?" Liz asked. "Do you mean rules?" She'd had enough rules to last a lifetime.

"Not rules, exactly. I was thinking more along the lines of, to love, honor and cherish. Do you think you could live with those guidelines?"

"Yes," she whispered. "Yes." She moved into the circle of his arms and caressed his cheek gently.

Evan smiled down at her. "I think we've both learned an important lesson here, don't you?"

"What's that?"

"Never judge a book by its cover."

Epilogue

"Now then, we've arranged for the flowers, the organist, and the soloist. I think we can move on to the reception." Vivian glanced up at her daughters. Kate nodded in agreement.

Liz gazed out the restaurant window, her chin propped in one hand. Idly, she stirred her tea, smiling to herself when the midday sunlight glinted off her engagement ring. The diamond glittered and shone. Soon she would be Mrs. Evan Delaford and she hugged that knowledge to her like a beloved security blanket.

In fact, she found she no longer had need of her old security blanket, the shapeless gray sweater. She and Evan gave it a proper burial several weeks ago, a mock solemn occasion, during which Evan's eulogy sent her into peals of laughter as they closed the lid of the garbage can.

Kate nudged Liz with an elbow. Vivian raised an eyebrow and Kate grinned. "What did I miss?" Truly, Liz was just as happy to have her mother and sister plan the bulk of her wedding. Being bogged down with too many details cut into her daydreaming time about her future as Evan's wife.

"The reception, dummy," Kate responded. "Get with the program, would you?"

"Ah, Kate," Liz sighed dramatically. "You just don't understand what it's like to be in love with Mr. Right. One of these days, you'll meet a tall, handsome—"

"Rich," Kate broke in.

"Stranger," Liz went on as though Kate hadn't spoken. "You'll fall in love—"

"Yeah, yeah, and then you and Mom can plan my wedding and reception while I admire my engagement ring and space out," Kate agreed.

"Reception?" Liz glanced at Vivian. "When did we start talking about the reception?"

Kate snorted. "Just now. Liz, wake up and help us make some decisions here. You don't want all of Evan's rich friends to think you can't throw together a simple reception for three hundred."

"Kate, dear." Vivian sent her younger daughter an admonishing glance. "Try to be more understanding. When it's your turn, we'll help you with your wedding plans. Won't we, Liz?"

Before Liz could respond, Kate spoke up. "Don't

hold your collective breath, you two. I'm not looking for Mr. Right, and I can pretty much guarantee he's not looking for me."

As she spoke her gaze caught that of a man seated at the end of the bar. He gave a friendly nod in her direction and Kate turned hastily away, but not before Liz noticed the exchange. Since Liz now invariably judged all men by the Evan Delaford standard, she found them all wanting. This one was, however, an excellent specimen, she had to admit. He was tall like Evan, and almost as well dressed, in a dark blue suit and maroon tie. He had straight black hair and serious dark eyes.

Giving her sister a return nudge, she nodded toward the bar. "Maybe that's him now," she whispered and they both started giggling when Vivian frowned.

"Girls. Can we please finish what we came for? Liz, you have to get back to work soon."

Vivian, having created ten new errands for herself in the process of planning Liz's reception, hurried off to complete them. Kate eyed her older sister. "Why didn't you tell Mom you had the afternoon off?"

Liz grinned. "So I could linger here and listen to your tale of woe for the thousandth time."

Kate frowned and began absently leafing through *The New York Times Book Review,* which Liz brought with her. "It's not a tale of woe, it's the story of my life. Laid off from the first real job I've had since college, getting dumped by the only guy I've been serious about since high school, and—"

"Moving back in with Mom." Liz chimed in.

She covered Kate's hand with one of her own. "It'll get better, Katie, you'll see. I bet you find a job in no time, and you'll get a place of your own. Maybe you'll even meet the man of your dreams." Liz lowered her voice as the man who had caught Kate's attention earlier walked by. He abruptly stopped and retraced his steps to their table.

"Excuse me," he said, addressing Kate who was still turning the pages of the *Book Review.* "Your name wouldn't be Liz by any chance, would it?"

Kate's gaze moved from him to Liz and back. "No, sorry, it's not," she answered.

He offered a self-deprecating grin. "Forgive me. It's just that I saw you looking at the *Book Review,* and I was hoping—never mind."

"No wait!" Liz nearly pounced on him as he turned to leave. She caught his sleeve, detaining him. "This sounds very intriguing. Please." She indicated the chair Vivian had recently vacated.

"It's not much of a story, really," he assured them as he took a seat. "Several weeks ago, I placed a personal ad." He noticed the look which passed between the two sisters. "I know, I know, I've heard stories about people who place those ads, but what can I say? I'm new to the area and it's hard to meet people in my line of work, so I figured, why not? What do I have to lose?

"Besides, one lady answered my ad who didn't sound like all the others." He glanced meaningfully at Kate. "Actually, I spoke with the woman's mother, but from what she told me, her daughter sounded like she had a brain. No offense," he added hastily, "but some of the women I've met over the years—some just live to shop and keep their manicure appointments. Anyway, this one sounded more like my type. Someone who reads, and can carry on a conversation about something other than herself. So I spoke to her mother, who sounded like a lovely woman—" he broke off when Kate and Liz burst into whole-hearted laughter.

"And let me guess," Liz continued the story for him when she was able, dabbing her eyes and avoiding those of her sister, "this lovely woman set up a meeting between you and her daughter. . . ." At his nod she went on, "here at Goodtimes for lunch. And you'd carry a copy of *The New York Times Book Review* with you so she could recognize you, right?"

"Right," he agreed eagerly. "In fact, that was the clincher. I figured any woman who reads the *Book Review* has to be my type."

"But for some reason, you didn't show up," Liz told him.

He seemed pleased at the way she had put it all together. "Wow, you're really sharp. That's exactly what happened. The entire electrical system on my new company car went," he snapped his fingers, "just like that on my way here. I was charging my cell phone through the cigarette lighter in the car, so that went, too. I was on the interstate about thirty miles away. No way to contact the restaurant to say I'd be late, and how could I, anyway? Her mother was supposed to find me. All I knew about the daughter was she had dark hair and green eyes . . . like you," he said, gazing at Liz.

"So your golden opportunity passed you by," Kate offered.

He shrugged good-naturedly and managed to look sheepish at the same time. "I had the mother's home phone number, but not with me. I figured I'd call later to explain what happened and try to set up another meeting. Unfortunately, I've recently adopted a puppy—a black lab," he added proudly. "And he likes to chew. He destroyed the pad I'd written all my notes on. And she never called back."

"But didn't you think it was weird that the mother made the arrangements in the first place?" Liz was dying to know the answer to that question.

"Well, yeah, sort of, but she made it all sound so logical. She said her daughter trusted her judgment, and had asked her to screen the callers. In fact, she made me feel pretty special about being the type of guy she'd approve of for her daughter."

When both Liz and Kate chuckled, he blushed. "I guess that sounds pretty stupid, huh?"

It was Kate who reached over and touched his sleeve. "No, not at all," she insisted. "It's really very sweet."

"You'll think this is even more ridiculous. Whenever I'm in the area, which is about once a week, I stop in here for lunch and bring a *Book Review* with me. Just in case." He glanced down at the magazine Kate had been perusing. "So you see why I had to ask . . ."

Liz stood abruptly. "I've got to run along, Mr. . . . ?" She looked at the man.

He stood and extended his hand. "I'm sorry. Joel. Joel Newman."

"Joel." She shook his hand. "It was lovely meeting you. And can I just say, I truly hope you find the woman of your dreams." She glanced meaningfully at her sister. "Bye, Katie." She bent close to her sister's ear. "See? Things are looking up already. Trust me, it's not such a bad thing to have Mom looking out for you."